Margaret Moyer

JAY COUNTY PUBLIC LIBRARY

materials are loaned for either 7 or 14

JAY COUNTY PUBLIC LIBRARY

1. Most library materials are loaned for
    three weeks and may be renewed once,
    so long as another person is not waiting
    for the material.

    3. Each borrower is responsible ry
    materials drawn on his card and for all fines accru-
    ing on the same.

Harvest of Love

HARVEST OF LOVE

NANCY SHEEHAN

AVALON BOOKS
THOMAS BOUREGY AND COMPANY, INC.
401 LAFAYETTE STREET
NEW YORK, NEW YORK 10003

© Copyright 1990 by Nancy Sheehan
Library of Congress Catalog Card Number: 90-82008
ISBN 0-8034-8820-3

PRINTED IN THE UNITED STATES OF AMERICA
BY HADDON CRAFTSMEN, SCRANTON, PENNSYLVANIA

To the memory of my mother,
Jessie May Pearman

Chapter One

As soon as she opened the front door, Darcy Lewis saw the green light blinking on her answering machine.

"Oh, no!" she muttered, tossing her large canvas shoulder bag over a nearby chair. She crossed the room and punched the rewind button.

It had been a long day, she thought as she watched the tape zip backward. She had been going since six this morning, and she desperately hoped that nothing had happened that would call her back to work. What she wanted now, she decided as she snapped on the listen button, was just to sit quietly on the front porch, one hand wrapped around a tall glass of lemon seltzer, and gaze out across the auburn fields. That was about all she could handle at this point.

"Ms. Lewis." The male voice was clear and resonant. "This is Dr. Randall, at Towering Oaks." Towering Oaks? But she had just come from Towering Oaks. And there wasn't any Dr. Randall there. "I'm calling in regard to the writing project. Could you give me a call?" This was

1

followed by a number and an extension and then a courteous, "Thank you."

Darcy jotted down the number as she waited to see if there were other messages. After she was sure that there were none, she ran the tape back and switched off the machine. In her bedroom she changed into jeans and a sweatshirt and headed out toward the kitchen.

Dr. Randall, she thought. Who on earth was Dr. Randall? And whoever he was, why on earth would he be calling her about the writing project? After all, she thought as she poured some seltzer over ice, the writing project had become one of her most successful projects. But, more important, who was this Dr. Randall?

She cut a thin slice of lemon and stuck it into her glass and then, turning toward the wall phone, she dialed a familiar number. Sue Gates answered on the second ring. They were close enough so that neither needed to identify herself on the phone, so Darcy got right to the point.

"Hi, Sue," she said. "Have you ever heard of a Dr. Randall?"

"As of this afternoon, yes. He was out at Towering Oaks for the first time, late today. Don't tell me he's gotten in touch with you already."

"As a matter of fact, yes. There was a message on the answering machine when I got home. He asked me to call him. He left a number—I think it's for St. Elizabeth—and an extension. Do you know what it's about?"

"He didn't give you any hint in his message?"

"Well, sort of. He said it was about the writing project, but I can't imagine why—"

Sue sighed. "Listen. I was going to call you tonight, anyway. Just thought I'd let you get home first, have a chance to unwind before—"

"Before what? What's this about, anyway?"

"Okay. I'll tell you what I know. Better sit down first, though."

Darcy pulled a stool over from the kitchen counter. "Okay. I'm sitting."

"This Dr. Randall—you're right. He is from St. Elizabeth—he's the new geriatrics doctor there. Made his first visit to Towering Oaks this afternoon—about an hour after you'd left. Anyway, he went around introducing himself and chatting with some of the residents, and it was all fine until he got to Louise Ryan."

Darcy sat up straight in the stool. "Why? What was wrong with Mrs. Ryan?"

"She was crying."

"Crying? But she was fine when I—"

"I know. Listen, I'd just been in her room myself, about twenty minutes earlier, to remind her about her blood-pressure medicine, and she'd been fine. She'd asked me to pull the shades and close the door so she could take a little nap. So

I did. Then when this Dr. Randall showed up for his first day, naturally I went with him—to introduce him to everyone and help him get acquainted with the place. And what should happen when we got to Louise Ryan's room? There she was, sitting by the window, shade still down, crying her heart out."

"Oh, no." Darcy rubbed her fingertips along her forehead. "But, Sue, I don't understand. Mrs. Ryan was great. She was laughing and having a fine time when I left—a little after four."

"I know, I know. I can't tell you how surprised I was. So, of course, I went over to her and asked what was wrong. She said she'd gotten to thinking about her family—her parents and her brothers and sisters. They're all dead now, you know. She's the last one left. And then she cried some more and said working on the writing project had gotten her to thinking about her husband. . . ."

"Oh, no." Darcy sighed. "I feel just terrible. I had no idea when I left. Otherwise, I would have stayed around, talked to her longer."

"I know you would have. Anyway, this Dr. Randall—and he's a nice guy, warm and sensitive—is a lot better than some of those doctors who come out there."

"Thank heavens for small favors," Darcy said dryly, remembering some run-ins she'd had with a couple of doctors from the city.

"So he sat down beside her. Took her hand, even, and in this very soft, gentle voice said, 'Louise, why are you so sad?' He was very nice about it. I've got to hand him that. Anyway, she said it was the writing project—that it got her to thinking about things, and then she talked for a while about her family and husband and all. He stayed with her until she had calmed down—just letting her talk. In fact, he didn't leave until she felt ready to go out to the lounge again.

"So I called one of the aides to wheel her down to where the others were. But when he and I were back in the hall, he really let loose. Started asking all these questions about the writing project—who was running it, what it was about, and so on. When I told him about you, he wanted to know who you were—what were your qualifications and all of that kind of thing.

"Naturally, I gave you a big buildup. Told him about your training and how good you are with the residents. But I could tell he was really ticked off. He kept saying the point of projects like yours was to make the residents feel better, not to leave them crying or depressed."

Darcy took a swallow of seltzer. "Well, of course," she said impatiently. "That goes without saying. After all, I don't go around trying to make people feel *worse,* for heaven's sake. The whole idea is to make them feel better." She paused and then lowered her voice. "I really feel awful about Mrs. Ryan, though! I never had any idea—"

"I know that, Darcy. I know how you feel about the residents, and I know how good you are. Listen, this wasn't anything you did. In fact, it was as much me as you. After all, I missed the cues from Louise Ryan too. It could have happened to anybody. It's just that sometimes the residents get really down. And even as caring as our staff is—and I think we're all pretty sensitive to the residents' needs—sometimes something like this will just slip by us."

Darcy rubbed her forehead. "I know. But even so. . . . Well, I still feel bad. I guess I just missed sensing Mrs. Ryan's mood." She hesitated. "Anyway, what else did this Dr. Randall say?"

"Oh, he just went on about how anyone running something like the writing project—and especially, he kept saying, anyone using autobiography—has a responsibility to stay with the patients afterward to avoid 'negative fallout,' as he kept calling it."

"Negative fallout! What an awful term!" Darcy paused. "Well, you know and I know that the writing project, and especially the autobiography project, has turned into a really successful program at Towering Oaks. In fact, I just started a group over at Good Shepherd, and it looks like it's going to go just as well." She hesitated. "Oh, I wish this hadn't happened! Honestly, I feel terrible about it. Whether this Dr. Randall got the wrong idea or not, I never wanted to leave Louise Ryan or anyone else upset. I had no idea." She was thoughtful for a moment. "Do you think I ought to run back over to Towering Oaks tonight and see her? See how she's doing?"

"I don't really think so, Darcy. I was there until five, and when I left, she was fine. You know, I think she just got sad, thinking about the past and all, and neither of us picked up on it. That sort of thing happens sometimes, in spite of everything. You know that."

Darcy sighed. "I suppose so. But I still feel terrible."

"Tell you what. Bet you haven't eaten yet, have you?"

"No."

"Why don't you go ahead, have some dinner? I'm going to do the same. Then let me call over there later on. Marie Watkins is on duty tonight. She's always good. I'll call her, see how Louise is doing. Then I'll give you a call back. Okay?"

Darcy nodded. "Okay."

"And look—don't worry about it. I was there all day. There was no way we could have known how upset Louise Ryan was. No matter how hard we try, these things do happen. So take off your shoes, have some dinner. . . . I'll get back to you later."

Darcy thanked her and hung up.

Out on the front porch, Darcy lifted her head to watch a flock of Canada geese move gracefully across the early autumn sky, their triangular formation unchanged as—like one—they headed toward a point just south of the setting sun. As usual they seemed to veer away from due south. Even as a little girl, she had noted that Canada geese always seemed to go a bit west in their autumn migration.

"Those birds are heading for Arizona," her grandmother had explained once when Darcy remarked about it. The two of them were sitting on the old porch glider that Grandma so loved, gently rocking back and forth as they watched the autumn sun set across the fields. "I can always tell. Some birds go to Florida for the winter, and some go to Tennessee or Mississippi, but Canada geese, they go to Arizona, New Mexico—nifty places like that." And Grandma had reached out, giving Darcy's hand a big squeeze. Darcy had giggled and snuggled closer to her. It was a common joke. When Grandma didn't know something, she'd come up with some outlandish explanation.

"Grandma, why do butterflies have all that striped color on their wings?"

"Why? Well, let me think. I guess it's so that when they're still in their cocoons, they can play chess on each other's wings." And Darcy would roar with laughter as Grandma chuckled and gave her a big hug.

Darcy finished her seltzer and stood up. It was hard to think about Grandma. Sometimes she just missed her so much. . . .

She headed back toward the kitchen to check on her dinner. After she finished talking to Sue, she had hastily thrown some leftover zucchini, a couple of carrots, and a bit of Cheddar cheese into a casserole. But then, when she put it into the oven, she had forgotten to set the timer or even glance at the clock. Now some fragrances were beginning to waft out from the oven, and she realized that her creation, however it might turn out, must be about done.

Darcy did a lot of her cooking that way. Not being much of a meat eater, she'd grab a couple of vegetables out of the refrigerator or, if the season was right, from her tiny vegetable garden, toss them together, add a few herbs, sometimes a can of mushroom soup and some leftover cheese, and then she'd mix them together in a casserole and let them bake until the concoction smelled right.

There were some disasters, of course—she would never forget the spinach leaf, cherry yogurt, and eggplant casserole—but most of the time they turned out fine. It was another knack she'd picked up from her grandmother, she remembered as she took the tiny casserole out of the oven and began scooping the steaming contents onto her plate.

She could just hear Grandma. "Let's see, Darcy—we have a beautiful red tomato, a perfect green pepper, some excellent Swiss cheese—oh, and here's an onion, and there's a package of whole-wheat noodles on the shelf. And I baked some fresh blueberry muffins this morning. Why, I'll bet we can make ourselves a fine meal!" And, of course, she would, Darcy remembered as she sat down at the kitchen table. No matter what odds and ends were lying around, Grandma could always make some kind of wonderful meal out of them.

Before eating, Darcy always closed her eyes for a moment of silence. Grandma had taught her that. "Never plunge right into your food," she'd say. "We're never so busy that we can't just stop for a moment and give thanks for what we have."

Oh, Grandma, how I miss you! Darcy thought as she sat at the kitchen table, her zucchini creation steaming on the plate before her. *Where are you? Where did you go? If only I could bring you back. . . .*

She opened her eyes and picked up her fork. *Not bad,* she thought as she took the first taste. Still hot but tasty. Grandma would be proud. Maybe if she put just a bit aside, she could take it in tomorrow. Maybe that would—

Silly! she told herself abruptly. *Grandma's gone. You know she's gone.* Darcy took another bite. Gone—but still, tomorrow, over at Good Shepherd Nursing Home, Darcy would stop and actually see Grandma again.

Darcy laid down her fork as her eyes began to fill. *Darn!* she told herself. *For heaven's sake, get a grip on yourself. After all, tomorrow is a full day.* Besides, she added as she slowly took another bite, not only did tomorrow mean Good Shepherd; tomorrow also meant calling and—who knows?—maybe even meeting this new Dr. Randall. She poured fresh, cold milk into a glass. She'd better get herself together. Tomorrow could be quite a day.

The eight-o'clock morning news was just getting underway as Darcy drove her red Ford Bronco into the Good Shepherd Nursing Home parking lot. She pulled in next to a sleek, gray Thunderbird, turned off the ignition, and stepped out the door.

As she walked briskly across the lot, her canvas shoulder bag hanging loosely over one shoulder, she wondered vaguely who owned the Thunderbird. She thought she knew all the staff members' cars. Perhaps one of the nurses had splurged over the weekend, she decided as she opened the side door and started down the long, familiar corridor.

As she approached the nurses' station, she could see a man standing by the high desk, obviously absorbed in something he was writing. *That's funny,* she thought. There were never visitors this early in the morning, and he certainly wasn't staff. Darcy knew all the staff, and she was sure she hadn't seen this man before. As she continued down the hall, she took a closer look.

He was about twenty-eight, maybe thirty, and he was tall—six feet, at least. He was wearing navy cords, white Reeboks, and a bright-blue, nubby-weave sweater that fell loosely around his hips. Beneath the sweater's crew neck, she could see a pin-striped shirt and red tie.

It was a casual outfit, but it set off his almost-perfect body in a way that made Darcy pause for a second and catch her breath. Beneath the loose-fitting sweater she could see the outline of his arms and shoulders, which were hard and muscular, like those of an experienced swimmer, and as she got closer, she noted that his hair was thick and dark brown. He looked up as she approached the nurses' station. His eyes were deep brown, like his hair, and the skin around the edges crinkled slightly as he looked up at her.

When she thought about it later, she was sure that she had intended just to sling her shoulder bag up on the desk and say something casual, like, "Hi, I'm Darcy Lewis," and maybe extend her hand in a cheerful greeting. But that wasn't what happened. Instead, she just stood there by the nurses' station, almost transfixed, like a teenager gazing at a TV star, unable to think of anything to say. He was, beyond all doubt, the handsomest man she had ever seen, and her heart did tiny cartwheels as their eyes met and locked.

After what seemed an eternity, he broke the spell as his face turned into a wide grin. "Good morning!" He extended his hand. "I'm Luke Randall."

Darcy set her shoulder bag on the desk. "And I'm Darcy Lewis." She held out her hand. His grasp was warm and firm, and it seemed as though he held her hand in his a bit longer than was usual.

"You must be on staff here." His eyes were warm and gentle, and Darcy had to struggle to keep her composure.

"Well, yes, as a matter of fact, I am. I'm a gerontology counselor. I come over to Good Shepherd every morning to work with some of the patients here."

Down the hall, she could see Fidella Ross, Good Shepherd's head day nurse, coming briskly toward the station. "Good morning, Darcy," Fidella said cheerfully as she took her place behind the desk. "I see you've met Dr. Randall—our new physician from St. Elizabeth's."

Even before Fidella finished her sentence, Darcy made the connection. Of course. Dr. Randall. The voice on the answering machine last night; the new geriatrics doctor over at Towering Oaks, the one who had talked to Sue Gates about Louise Ryan.

She turned and faced him squarely. Time to forget those warm brown eyes, she told herself sternly, that strong, muscular build, that faint, masculine scent. This was the doctor who didn't like the writing project, who thought she caused trouble for the residents. This guy could mean trouble.

"I'm sorry," she said evenly as she struggled to ignore the giddy feelings that were going on inside her. "I didn't make the connection right away." He seemed startled. "I think you left a message on my answering machine yesterday. I was planning to return your call this morning."

He furrowed his brow for a second, clearly puzzled. "Call?"

"Yes." She looked away. Those eyes of his made it hard to concentrate. And then there was that faint, disturbing whiff of lemon-lime hovering in the air—probably an after-shave lotion, she thought. "From Towering Oaks. Didn't you call me from Towering Oaks yesterday?"

His eyes narrowed slightly as he looked at her more closely. "Oh, you also work at Towering Oaks?"

Darcy nodded.

He shook his head. "Of course. You're Ms. Lewis. I've got the connection now. Yes, I did call you yesterday." He stepped back slightly and cleared his throat. "I'm sorry. I guess I didn't realize that you were on staff at both places—Towering Oaks and Good Shepherd."

"Yes. I split my time between the two—mornings here at Good Shep and afternoons at Towering Oaks."

"I see." He turned back toward the nurses' station. "Mrs. Ross, I wonder if you could fit in a little more activity for Cordelia Campanella." He glanced down at his clipboard. "Room 117. She seems a bit depressed. I checked her over. Everything's okay, but her spirits are down." He shook his head. "That always concerns me."

"Yes, Doctor." Fidella took the clipboard he held out to her. "But, of course," she said, nodding toward Darcy, "this is the lady you should talk to about that. Darcy plans most of the activities for the patients. And if someone is really down, Darcy is a lifesaver. I've seen her spend hours with a depressed patient." She smiled warmly. "Darcy's really wonderful."

"Thanks, Fidella," Darcy said quietly. It was always good to hear such warm praise.

"Yes, well, I've already heard something of Ms. Lewis's work." Darcy wondered if she detected just a touch of irony in his comment. He reached across the desk and pulled the clipboard back toward him. "Perhaps she and I need to talk a bit more." He scribbled a few more notes and returned the clipboard to Fidella's side of the desk.

"Let's see," he said, turning toward Darcy. He was all business now. The warm smile, the crinkle around the brown eyes were both gone. He glanced at his watch. "I have rounds back at St. Elizabeth Hospital at eight-thirty. But I'll be over at Towering Oaks this afternoon. Will you be there today, Ms. Randall?"

Darcy pulled herself up to her fullest height. The top of her head barely reached his chin. "As a matter of fact, yes," she answered briskly. "I'm at Towering Oaks every day, Monday through Friday, from one to four."

"Good. Perhaps we can find time to talk then." He turned back to Fidella. "I think the rest of my orders are clear, Mrs. Ross. But if there are questions, you know how to reach me."

"Yes, Doctor." Fidella nodded and immediately began filing the orders with each patient's chart.

"What do you think of him?" she asked after the tall figure of Dr. Randall had retreated down the hall and out toward the parking lot.

Darcy shrugged nonchalantly. "Okay—I guess. I really don't know a lot about him."

"Yeah. I gathered you'd just met. But then he just started at St. Elizabeth's on Monday. Yesterday was his first day here."

"Same at Towering Oaks. I talked to Sue Gates last night. She told me something about him."

Fidella turned back to the charts. "Everyone says he's really good. Got great credentials. He's already finished one residency, you know—in internal medicine at University Hospital in Chicago. And now he's finishing his second, over at St. Elizabeth's—in geriatrics. Couldn't be better," she added quietly.

"No, I guess not." Out in the parking lot, Darcy could see the little gray Thunderbird taking off. *So that's who it belongs to,* she thought. She turned back toward Fidella. "Listen—it's okay if I leave my things here, isn't it, while I run down to ARD?"

Fidella glanced up. "I figured that was why

you were here so early. You wanted to squeeze in an extra visit before you start work this morning." She smiled gently. "No problem. I'll keep an eye on your things."

"Thanks, Fidella. I won't be long." And she turned and headed down toward the wing at the far end of the hall.

The white cotton spread barely covered the frail figure who lay propped up on the hospital bed, her tiny head pointed in the general direction of the TV, where a jovial weatherman was cracking jokes and discussing a colorful map.

Darcy walked softly across the room. "Hi, Grandma," she said softly.

The little head remain fixed toward the TV. Darcy could see her face now. There was a trace, just a trace, of a dim, uncomprehending smile as she watched the portly weatherman cavort around the set.

Darcy stood beside her, looking gently down at the bony little face that she had loved so much for so long. "Grandma?" She spoke a bit louder than before. Sometimes she had to do that—just to get her grandmother's attention. "It's Darcy, Grandma. How are you today?"

The little face slowly turned toward her, the eyes blank. As usual, there was no sign of recognition.

"Oh, hello, Nurse." Her voice was weak and gravelly. "I'm fine." She turned her head slowly back toward the TV.

"No, Grandma, it's Darcy." There was no answer, no response. "Can I get you something, Grandma? Maybe I could get you your breakfast." She was grasping for something to talk about even though she knew perfectly well that all the patients at Good Shepherd had been fed by eight. "Have you had breakfast yet, Grandma?"

Silence. Darcy turned toward the TV. The weatherman was doing a commercial for some dog food. As he talked, he placed a bowl down on the floor, next to a ravenous dachshund. Her grandmother gave a weak laugh.

Encouraged, Darcy turned back toward the bed. "Isn't that a cute dog, Grandma?" She glanced at the TV. The dog was frantically licking the last trace of food from the dish. "Just look at him eat."

Her grandmother said something, but Darcy couldn't make it out. She leaned closer to the bed. "What, Grandma? I didn't hear you."

Her grandmother lifted a bony hand and weakly pointed toward the TV. "Char-lee," she said faintly.

Charlie. Of course. That was the name of the dog the family had had years ago—long before

Darcy was born. But through the years Grandma had talked so much about Charlie that Darcy had grown up thinking of him as a dear, departed family member.

"The dog reminds you of Charlie, Grandma? Is that what you said?"

Her grandmother slowly looked back at her and nodded. Then she stopped and stared at Darcy for several seconds. "Hello, Laura," she said faintly. "I haven't seen you for a long time."

Darcy sighed. Laura was her mother. She'd been dead for more than twenty years now—killed in an automobile accident, along with Darcy's father, when Darcy was six years old. But for her grandmother, all the years between now and then had been forgotten.

Like most patients with Alzheimer's disease, her grandmother had lost all of her recent memories. Her daughter's tragic death, the years of bringing up Darcy, and, in fact, even Darcy's very existence had long since slipped from her consciousness. For her grandmother, it was as though those decades hadn't even happened. Even Grandpa, who had died a year before the accident, rarely got mentioned anymore. Only her very oldest memories remained.

"I'm not Laura, Grandma," Darcy said gently. "I'm Darcy. I was in to see you on Saturday. Remember?" She leaned over and gave the tiny figure a hug. "But I'm glad you're feeling better today."

As usual, there was no response, but Darcy was accustomed to that. Slowly her grandmother turned her attention back to the TV. "Good-bye, Laura," she said finally. "Have a nice day at school, dear." She closed her eyes and began to doze.

Darcy bent over and gently kissed her grandmother's forehead. "Good-bye, Grandma. I'll stop by again in a couple of days."

But except for the quiet breathing, there was no response. Darcy gave her grandmother's hand a gentle squeeze and quietly left the room.

There was no point in staying longer. She knew that. She didn't even know whether her many visits did any good; there was no way of telling. She thought they did, and, certainly, she hoped they did. But either way, she told herself as she headed back down the corridor, short, regular visits were the only thing left that she could still give her grandmother.

Well, not quite, she reminded herself as she saw some of the patients slowly walking or being wheeled into the large, airy dayroom. Perhaps there was nothing more that she could do for Grandma, but there was certainly plenty that she could do for other elderly people.

At the end of the hall she recognized Roy

Bogan, sitting in his wheelchair and waving happily at her as she approached the dayroom.

"Good morning, Mr. Bogan," she called cheerfully. He beamed in return.

Darcy was about to begin her day. And, like every other workday, it would be a day of partial dedication. Not that Darcy didn't love her work—in fact, she adored it. But her work filled more than one need in her life.

First of all, it was a job and one that she thoroughly enjoyed. But it was also something more. Because it was through her work that Darcy was attempting to pay her debt—her debt to her grandmother. For when her parents had been so tragically killed, it had been Grandma who had taken Darcy in, brought her up, and showered her with all the love and care that a child could want.

Now Grandma was gone, or almost gone. ARD. Alzheimer's and Related Disorders—the mysterious disease with no cure, the sickness that took over the brain and devoured it, robbing it of memories and coherence and destroying even its victim's very sense of self.

The Long Good-bye, someone had called it. As soon as she first heard the term, Darcy had understood it exactly. She had begun her own good-bye to Grandma almost four years ago, when the disease first made itself known. In slightly less than a year the Grandma she had known and loved for so long had begun to fade. She was there—and yet she wasn't.

Even now, Grandma was alive; some fragile part of her lingered on. Darcy had just seen that part. But the other part of Grandma—the Grandma who had loved her, joked with her, given her hugs—that Grandma was gone. She was nowhere to be found. And yet, how could someone be part here and part not here? What strange twist of fate had taken that wonderful, fun-loving part of her grandmother away and yet left behind this frail, emaciated other part? Darcy would never understand.

But then, there were these other men and women, the patients who *were* still here—weak and frail, perhaps, but still very much alive—and it was to them and to others like them that Darcy had decided to devote her life.

She never talked about it, never told anyone. But that, she reminded herself as she approached the busy morning stir of the dayroom, was why she had chosen gerontology as her lifework. It had become like a mission to her. It was her way of saying thanks to Grandma.

Chapter Two

Shortly after noon Darcy left Good Shepherd and headed over to Towering Oaks Retirement Village where she worked every afternoon. How different the two places were, she thought as she pulled the red Bronco into the indoor parking area beneath the sleek, modern building. Where Good Shepherd was small and homelike, a nursing home devoted totally to caring for those too frail to continue to care for themselves, Towering Oaks was large and modern, offering facilities both for those who needed full-time care as well as for those who were still relatively independent but who craved the companionship, amenities, and security of assisted living.

When Darcy had finally faced the fact, three years ago, that her grandmother would have to enter a facility with full-time care, it had not been easy for her to choose between Towering Oaks and Good Shepherd. In its own particular way, each home was excellent, with a fine, caring staff.

But Good Shepherd, which was church operated, had a homeyness and a personal touch that appealed to Darcy, and it was to Good Shepherd that, with considerable reluctance and no small amount of guilt, she had finally taken her grandmother. And since she now was as reconciled as she ever would be to her grandmother's need for around-the-clock care, there were no lingering doubts in her mind that she had made the right decision. As much as she admired and respected the care given in the large nursing wing at Towering Oaks, with its high-tech equipment and state-of-the-art treatment, she had never regretted her choice. After all, there was no need now for Grandma to have access to heroic measures. Quite the opposite. What Grandma needed most now was a small, warm environment with friendly faces and a lot of TLC.

"The writing group is waiting for you," Sue Gates said as Darcy came down the long, spotless corridor. "There's been a lot of excitement about it all morning. Everyone's looking forward to it."

"Great! I was working with a small reminiscence group over at Good Shepherd earlier. Everyone seemed to like it there too." She hesitated. "But what about Louise Ryan? How is she doing?"

Late last evening Sue had called back to report that Mrs. Ryan was in good spirits and seemed completely recovered from the afternoon depression that had so alarmed Dr. Randall. But Darcy still had the matter on her mind. And, of course, her brief encounter with Dr. Randall over at Good Shepherd this morning had only increased her nervousness.

"Louise is fine. In fact, she's probably down in the Seminar Room by now, waiting for you."

"Terrific!" Darcy gave a wave and headed down the hall toward the elegant oak-paneled Seminar Room where the writing group met.

The room was buzzing as she walked in. About ten residents were sitting around the long table that stretched down the middle of the room, two more than yesterday. A couple were sitting in wheelchairs, comfortably situated at the large seminar table, various sections of which were especially designed to accommodate wheelchairs, while others were sitting on chairs, some with crutches or walkers safely held within a protruding rim that was conveniently located on the side of each chair.

"Hi, everybody," Darcy said as she entered the room. Of all the many parts of her job, working with small groups was one of her favorites.

"Hello, Darcy," several of the patients said while others waved cheerful greetings.

Darcy fished in her shoulder bag for her pen and notebook and then took a seat along the side of the oak table, situating herself in a vacant space between Helen-Marie Wiggins and Wadsworth Logan. Whenever she worked with groups, she always avoided sitting at the head of the table. She didn't want to act like a teacher or even to leave the impression that she thought she knew more than they did. Darcy was well aware of the wisdom that came with age, and she was genuinely respectful of each patient's considerable store of knowledge.

"So. . . ." She looked around the room with a smile. "Who's going to start today?"

There were several seconds of silence as the participants looked around anxiously. "I will," Henry Van Dusen said, clearing his throat gruffly.

"Great!" Darcy leaned back in her chair, delighted. During the writing group's first few meetings, Mr. Van Dusen had been the curmudgeon of the group. Abrupt and surly, he had shown no interest in contributing—only in listening, that sour expression never leaving his face.

"It's a poem," he announced sternly and then stopped and looked suspiciously around the room, as though he expected someone to step in and object. When he saw only eager faces, he cleared his voice and began:

Today I saw a leaf fall
Against a clear, blue sky.

But August—why a fallen leaf?
I asked as it drifted by.

He hesitated and looked around. The group sat
listening attentively.

But August means September
And September brings us fall,
And fall means leaves begin to change—
It's that way for us all.

And so I sat and watched the leaf,
My mind alive and free.
The seasons change, but life goes on—
That's how it's meant to be.

There was a brief silence, and then the group
broke into spontaneous applause. "Very
nice. . . ." "Very good. . . ." "Just lovely," several
of the participants said together. "Excellent
poem, Henry," Wadsworth Logan, beside Darcy,
murmured appreciatively.

"It is, Mr. Van Dusen. It's a beautiful poem."

Although most of the patients called Darcy by
her first name, Darcy made it a point never to
initiate the practice herself. She knew that it was
not uncommon, in geriatrics, to automatically
address all older people by their first names. But
Darcy had thought this matter over at length. Be-

cause she maintained a strong belief in the dignity of older persons, she genuinely believed that each patient had a right to decide whether to invite others into a first-name relationship. And, bearing in mind her own youth, she was always particularly careful not to take it upon herself to make that overture.

She looked around the room. Her eyes fell on Louise Ryan, the lady about whom Dr. Randall had been so disturbed last evening. But now, as she watched her, Mrs. Ryan seemed in fine spirits.

Tentatively, Darcy put out a feeler. "How about it, Mrs. Ryan? Have you had a chance to do any more on your autobiography?"

Louise Ryan smiled shyly. "As a matter of fact, I have, Darcy." She looked tentatively around the room. "You see, yesterday afternoon, after we met, I was feeling sort of down. I guess I just got a bit sad—you know, after all that reminiscing." The group nodded sympathetically. "But then last night, when most of you were down in the TV room, I went into the library and worked—for at least two hours, I guess." She beamed proudly. "I'd like to read it to you. . . ." She looked around the room. "That is, if you'd like to hear it," she added softly.

"Oh, yes. . . ." "Indeed we would. . . ." "Let us hear it, Louise," several members said.

Mrs. Ryan looked down at the yellow pad before her and took a deep breath. Then, very softly, she began reading.

It was the second chapter of her autobiography. The first chapter, which she had read yesterday, had dealt with her earliest memories, her childhood on the Illinois prairie around the time of World War I.

The second chapter told about beginning first grade. With clear images and a light, free-flowing style, Mrs. Ryan told about her teacher, Miss Witherington, and her own first day in the little one-room schoolhouse. Her images were as clear as if the event had happened yesterday, Darcy thought, and her anecdotes held the group spellbound. As she described the old wooden desks, with the inkwells in the corner and the lift-up tops, all deeply etched with students' names and funny drawings, the group chuckled. But when she wrote about a favorite uncle who, during a January blizzard, had gone out to search for a runaway colt and later had been found, in a nearby woods, frozen to death, several of the listeners began fumbling for tissues.

When Mrs. Ryan finished, Darcy glanced around the room quickly. There was not a dry eye anywhere, including, she realized, her own. It was a well-written, deeply moving chapter, and

Darcy was sure that it was one of the best pieces of work to come out of the writing group yet.

Still dabbing at their eyes, the group's members showered Mrs. Ryan with praise. "It was wonderful, Louise." "It really took me back to my own first grade." "And that blizzard! My goodness, Louise—I almost felt cold, just listening to you describe it!"

Darcy watched Louise Ryan closely. She wanted to be sure that if there was any "negative fallout," to use Dr. Randall's term, she picked up on it. But as she sat there, listening to the surrounding praise, Mrs. Ryan beamed.

To be sure, Darcy noted, her eyes were shimmering a bit, but Darcy was sure that this was as much from tears of joy as from any sadness she might feel. Still, she watched closely as, in the midst of the continued praise, Mrs. Ryan reached for another tissue.

A knock on the door interrupted the enthusiastic discussion. That was odd, Darcy thought as she got to her feet to answer. Unless summoned, the staff never interrupted group work.

"Hi, Ms. Lewis. Nurse Gates told me you were here." The dark-brown eyes of Dr. Luke Randall smiled gently into her own. "I wonder if you would mind if I came in and joined you and the group for a while."

For just a second Darcy caught her breath. *No*

man, she thought, *should be this handsome.* But then her thoughts quickly returned to the writing group. What a moment for him to come around!

She glanced helplessly over her shoulder at the participants, many of whom were still teary eyed and clinging to tissues. Terrific. Dr. Randall already had suspicions about her competence. And now, barging in at this moment, he was going to get some really great impressions about her work with groups. *Darn!* she thought in frustration. Why did he have to come now, of all times?

Behind her, Helen-Marie Wiggins called out a cheerful, "Hello, Dr. Randall."

"Hi, Doc," Henry Van Dusen said in his usual gruff tone.

"Come on in, Doctor," Louise Ryan said, an audible catch still lingering in her voice.

Darcy pursed her lips. There were no words to express her frustration. But at the same time, she reminded herself, what choice did she have? After all, he *was* the doctor, and around here doctors had the last word. Besides, it looked as though the patients all liked him. None of them seemed to see his arrival as an intrusion.

"Why, of course, Doctor," she said with forced politeness. "How nice of you to drop by! Of course. We'd just love to have you come and join us," and with an exaggerated sweep of her hand, she stood aside to let him enter.

Several of the participants, still dabbing at their eyes, began to move to make room for him at the table.

"No, no," Dr. Randall demurred. "I don't want to interrupt anything."

Darcy groaned inwardly. *No, not much you don't,* she thought grimly. Putting everything together—the message on her answering machine, her phone conversation with Sue Gates the night before, and the early-morning encounter over at Good Shepherd—it seemed pretty clear that Dr. Randall had questions about her work, suspected that she might be needlessly upsetting patients, and—who knows?—might even be hurting them in some way.

As she returned to her place along the side of the table, Darcy smiled cheerfully. But inside she was furious at Dr. Randall's intrusion, at his obvious suspicion of her competence, and maybe even of her intentions. In addition, of course, his timing was wretched. Half the members were still wiping away tears.

"Oh, Dr. Randall, you should have heard Henry Van Dusen's poem. It was just beautiful," Mrs. Wiggins said, still dabbing at her eyes. "And Louise Ryan's autobiography! It's so touching!"

He found a chair along one side of the room and sat down. "I'd love to hear them." He leaned back and placed a Reeboked foot over his knee as he glanced casually around the room.

Although he was clearly trying to project an offhand look, Darcy was sure that those dark-brown eyes were not missing a trick. In fact, even from where she sat, she could see him taking careful note of the pile of wadded tissues in front of Mrs. Wiggins, the noise as Henry Van Dusen loudly blew his nose, and the obvious redness around Louise Ryan's eyes. *Great,* Darcy told herself, *just great.*

He looked up and smiled benignly across the table at Darcy. "Please don't let me interrupt you, Ms. Lewis. Do continue."

Darcy cleared her throat. *Right,* she told herself. *Just continue right along.* Just as though everything she said and everything she did weren't going to be watched like a hawk for the rest of the session!

She looked around the room cheerfully. "Well," she said, trying to conceal her nervousness, "so who wants to go next?"

Silence.

"How about it, folks?"

No answer. Now she was getting anxious. Suppose no one spoke up? Then Dr. Randall *really* would wonder about what was going on in her groups.

"Who wants to read?" Darcy asked as her eyes

nervously swept around the table. Surely someone would come forward.

Out of the side of one eye, she caught a gesture
from Wadsworth Logan. He was in his early
eighties and, because of a stroke, was confined to
a wheelchair.

"Mr. Logan?" she asked hopefully. "How
about you?"

Wadsworth had mentioned an idea for a short
story to the group yesterday. It had sounded
quite good, Darcy thought—a dog story based on
something that had happened to him as a boy.
Maybe he'd have the beginning of his story ready
for today. Darcy hoped so.

Wadsworth was absolutely solid. Like a rock,
Darcy thought. He took life as it came, never
complaining, relying, instead, on a sharp sense
of humor to get him over the rough spots. His
story had to be good, Darcy figured, and probably even funny too. Something like that would
really help lighten things up a bit. In fact, in Dr.
Randall's critical eyes, a story by Wadsworth
Logan might just redeem the whole purpose of
the writing group.

"Did you get a chance to do any more on your
story?" she asked eagerly.

Wadsworth shifted his position uncomfort-
ably. "Yes, Darcy, as a matter of fact, I did." He

hesitated. "But I'm not sure whether it's ready for reading yet."

Several of the participants spoke at once. "Oh, come on, Wadsworth. Let us hear it." "Yes, we'd really like to." "You're too modest, Wadsworth. Come on."

Wadsworth looked over the top of his reading glasses at Dr. Randall, who was sitting across from him, along the far side of the room, and then he glanced at Darcy.

"Go ahead, Mr. Logan," she said gently. "The group would really like to hear it."

"Well, all right." He pulled a manila folder out of the side pocket of his wheelchair and laid it on the table before him. "You probably remember from yesterday that this story is based on a true incident—something that happened to me the year that I turned ten."

Everyone nodded.

"Its title is 'Brief Valor.' "

The group murmured approvingly.

Wadsworth stopped to wipe his glasses and then, after clearing his throat, he began to read.

The story was about a dog named Chep who had lived all his life on a farm with his master, a boy named Len, and Len's parents. The story opened with some humorous anecdotes about Len and Chep. One scene described Chep following Len to school every morning and then waiting out in the play yard for him, and another told of Len bringing Chep into his room at night after Len's parents were asleep and how Chep would sleep with his head on the pillow, right next to Len's. By this time Wadsworth had firmly established that the boy and the dog were as one.

Darcy was delighted. The group was chuckling warmly, and everyone seemed to be enjoying the story. Even Dr. Randall, she noted, was listening enthusiastically, those handsome eyes crinkling as he smiled.

Wadsworth moved on to an incident at a local swimming hole. The boy Len had gone swimming alone. He knew he wasn't supposed to go into the water alone. But it was a very hot day, and there was no one around. Len was having a fine time, diving and swimming while Chep lay in the shade along the side of the swimming hole, panting and trying to stay cool as he patiently watched his young master frolicking in the water.

Unexpectedly, while out over his head, Len got a cramp. He couldn't move. He screamed for help, but there was no one around to hear. Panicked, he could feel himself starting to go under. He was terrified. But then, just as everything began to go black, there was Chep, swimming frantically toward him. In desperation Len grabbed Chep's collar, and, heroically, Chep dragged Len safely to shore. But the heat and exertion were too much for the old dog, and a few minutes later he was lying lifelessly beside Len. Chep had died saving his young master.

Wadsworth laid the manuscript down on the table and fumbled for his handkerchief. "Please excuse me, folks, but just remembering. . . ." And he broke off to blow his nose loudly.

Across from him, Helen-Marie Wiggins dabbed at her eyes as she sadly shook her head. "Oh, that's so sad, so sad."

From the end of the table, Henry Van Dusen spoke gruffly. "I had a dog just like that. Died the very day I turned twelve." He pulled out his handkerchief. "And to this day, I still miss that dog—best friend I ever had."

Louise Ryan wiped her eyes sadly. "Oh, Wadsworth, that was such a touching story!"

"It was, it was," several of the other participants said together.

"But it was *so* sad," Helen-Marie Wiggins said as she quickly reached for another tissue.

Next to her, Louise Ryan suddenly buried her face in her hands, her body shaking with gentle sobs. "Oh, it just isn't fair," she said softly. "He was such a good dog. . . ."

"Better than a lot of people," Henry Van Dusen said sourly.

Louise Ryan began weeping quietly. "Why do these things have to happen, anyway? I just don't understand. . . ." And she buried her face in the tissue as she continued to sob.

Darcy pushed her chair back and quickly made her way to Mrs. Ryan's side. But even before Darcy had reached her, Dr. Randall's voice shot across the room, quietly but authoritatively.

"Ms. Lewis, press the staff button, please."

Darcy stopped and looked at him in surprise. There was a staff button in every room, but it was intended for emergency use only.

In a flash he was on his feet and striding across the room. "I said"—his voice was firm but low— "push the staff button." And before she could move, he had reached the button and pushed it himself.

Within seconds Sue Gates and two nurse's aides were in the room.

"Mrs. Gates. . . ." Dr. Randall's voice was loud and firm. "I think the residents have had enough of the writing project for today. Would you and the aides please see that they are escorted back to the dayroom?"

"But wait a minute, Doc," Wadsworth said in surprise. "We're not through yet. I wanted to get the group's reaction to my story. I don't even know yet if they liked—"

"I'm sorry, Mr. Logan. I'm sure that Ms. Lewis can arrange for you to get some feedback

tomorrow. For today, however, I think it's time
to call things quits."

Sue Gates shot Darcy an astonished look, and
then she and the aides began helping the patients
out of the room, some of them still protesting.

Darcy stood by the side of the table, helplessly
watching her group dissolve. *How dare he!* she
thought angrily. There were no words to express
her outrage.

When the room was empty, she walked over
and faced him. He was standing by the door,
watching the last of the residents making their
way down toward the TV room.

Her voice was trembling with rage as she
spoke. "What in the world are you doing, Doctor?" she asked quietly. "There was nothing
wrong there. That group was doing fine."

He turned toward her. "Fine!" he exploded.
"Nothing wrong! Good heavens! You have the
patients all upset, half the room is in sobs, the
other half is buried in Kleenex, and you say nothing's wrong?"

"Dr. Randall, I could have taken care of it. If
you'd just let me—"

"Taken care of it? Right!" His voice was heavy
with sarcasm. "I think I already have a taste of
your idea of taking care of things." He turned toward the door. "From now on, Ms. Lewis, you
can consider your writing group done, canceled,

over, out. . . ." He angrily turned back to her. "Do I make myself clear?"

Darcy looked directly at him, her lips firmly pursed. How could she ever have thought that his eyes were warm and gentle? What on earth had made her think he was so all-fired handsome? She turned away from him quickly. She absolutely detested him.

"Yes, Doctor," she muttered grimly.

"Good!" he shot back as he turned and headed out the door and down the hall.

"I hear you had a first-class run-in over at Towering Oaks yesterday," Fidella Ross said as Darcy approached the nurses' station at Good Shepherd early the next morning.

"Did I ever!" Darcy heaved her shoulder bag up on the desk. "This Dr. Randall is really something else. . . ."

"That's what Sue Gates said. I talked to her last night." Fidella tapped a small stack of manila folders into a neat pile. "Sue was furious. Said he was talking about canceling all of the writing groups—even the one over here at Good Shepherd."

Darcy nodded. "I talked to Sue last night, and that's what she told me too. You see, after the run-in yesterday—that is, after this Dr. Randall came barging into the writing group, uninvited, mind you—and then, five minutes later, he's shouting, 'Hit the staff button, hit the staff button. . . .' " Darcy stopped in frustration. "Honestly, Fidella, every time I think of it, I get so darn mad. The nerve of that guy! Who does he think he is? He's—what? Maybe three weeks into geriatrics? And already he thinks he's some big-shot expert. Knows everything." She rubbed her forehead in frustration. "Honestly! What a jerk!"

Fidella propped her elbows up on the desk and rested her chin in her palms. "Yeah. Well, you know what the trouble is, don't you?"

Darcy looked at her questioningly.

"This is just my opinion, of course. So I could be wrong."

"No, go ahead," Darcy urged her. "What do you think is going on? What's *wrong* with this man?"

"I think he's just had too much training in internal medicine. He did his residency at University Hospital, you know."

Darcy nodded. Chicago's University Hospital was considered one of the best in the country, with an especially strong department in internal medicine.

"Great hospital but they don't have a lot of geriatrics there. I mean, not the way we do. The patients at University Hospital are all sick, really sick. That's why they're there. It's not like out in the nursing homes. Here the patients aren't always that ill—you know that. Some of our patients may have had strokes, and all of them are just too frail to continue to take care of themselves. But that doesn't necessarily make them really sick."

"So you think—"

"I think that Dr. Randall's residency in internal medicine is standing in the way of his understanding geriatrics. He looked at your writing group, and from what Sue told me, I gather there were some emotional responses. . . ."

Darcy nodded grimly.

"And so, right away, like the good medical doctor that he is, he thought, 'Aha! Stress! Get this woman'—meaning you, of course—'get this woman away from my patients!' Because, remember, Darcy, in a place like University Hospital, you can't permit unnecessary stress. You can't allow a lot of negative emotions to enter the patients' lives. Those patients are too sick for that. I know. I've worked there. So the staff is taught to deliberately protect the patients from stress. They limit visiting hours, put restrictions on who can come in and who can't, and generally they try to keep the patients' lives as tranquil and quiet as they can." She paused. "They have to. Otherwise, the patients may not heal."

Darcy looked at her thoughtfully. "So you think maybe that's what happened in the writing group? He came in and saw some emotion and—"

"And immediately thought, 'Stress! Call the staff! Call the aides! Get the patients out of here. Too much stress!' And, of course, he doesn't understand that those patients are not all that sick. And the writing project isn't really stressful, anyway." She paused. "In fact, personally, I think it's a great project. Helps the patients to stay mentally active, to be productive, to get together and discuss recollections and ideas—it's wonderful."

Darcy was quiet for a moment. "That's really helpful, Fidella. I never thought of it that way. It seemed to me that the man had gone suddenly crazy. I never thought of it as too much—"

"Too much medical model. Too much following the procedures of a big-city hospital. Geriatrics is different, you know. It takes a lot more humanity but a lot less strict medical practice." Fidella paused. "That's probably why I like it so much. It's a warm, friendly branch of medicine—not cold and sterile like some of the big-city hospitals."

Darcy watched her friend thoughtfully. "I'm really glad you've reminded me of all this, Fidella. It helps to give me a perspective on the whole thing." She glanced at her watch. "But, in view of everything, what about the writing group here today, at Good Shepherd? Do you think I ought to go ahead with it?"

Fidella smiled as she leaned conspiratorially across the desk. "Listen, Darcy, I'm head nurse here, and nobody's told *me* to cancel your writing group. What Dr. Randall may have told Sue Gates over at Towering Oaks—well, what can I say! That's Towering Oaks and this is Good Shep. He hasn't told me anything. So as far as I'm concerned, it's business as usual. The writing group is expecting you at nine, and I say, go to it."

Darcy picked up her bag and flung it on her shoulder. "Thanks, Fidella." She turned and started briskly down the hall. "But if you-know-who happens to come in to make rounds while I'm in the meeting room—well, get the troops ready. He'll probably be ringing emergency buttons and everything else to get the group stopped."

"Yeah," Fidella called after her. "And he thinks *you're* the one causing the stress!"

But the writing group at Good Shepherd went well, with no intrusion or interruption. There were two fine poems, several stories, and the beginning of an autobiography.

When it was over, Darcy hurried down to the

ARD wing for a few minutes with her grand-mother. The TV was on, but, as often happened, her grandmother showed no awareness of Darcy's presence. One of the nurses was there, preparing Grandma for a ride in her wheelchair out to an adjacent terrace.

Perhaps Grandma was just distracted, Darcy thought as she walked back down the hall. But as she opened the door and headed out across the parking lot, she knew that it wouldn't have mattered whether the nurse was there or not, whether the TV was on or off. It didn't matter what was going on around her. Grandma simply no longer knew that Darcy existed. Grandma had forgotten all about her.

Chapter Three

As soon as Darcy pulled into the sleek, underground parking area at Towering Oaks that afternoon, she saw the gray Thunderbird parked along one side of the lower level. Great! That was all she needed—to have another fun encounter with Dr. Luke Randall!

Rather than go up on the elevator, which opened directly on to the nurses' station, Darcy decided to go out and across the lawn and in the side door. That way she might be less likely to run into him, a meeting she definitely did not need at this point.

As she approached the side entrance, she saw a couple of residents sitting side by side on one of the lawn love seats, deeply involved in conversation. As she got closer, she recognized Wadsworth Logan and Louise Ryan. They were holding hands, she noted, and their faces were almost touching as they talked. That was interesting, she thought. She hadn't realized that they were such good friends. But rather than disturb them,

47

Darcy simply veered over toward another side door and entered there.

Sue Gates was coming up the hall. "Hi, Darcy. What brings you in this entrance?"

Briefly Darcy explained how she was hoping to avoid another meeting with Luke Randall. She also mentioned how she had come upon Louise Ryan and Wadsworth Logan out on the side terrace.

Sue nodded. "I know. Those two have been together a lot lately." She smiled. "It's sort of neat. It looks like they're becoming great friends. But since you've mentioned Dr. Randall, I might as well tell you. He was asking about you earlier."

"Oh?"

"Yeah. Wanted to know if you'd been in yet today. Said he hoped to see you."

Darcy grimaced. "To scream at me some more, I suppose."

Sue reached out and touched Darcy's shoulder. "I don't know, but you'll soon find out." She nodded down the hall. "Here comes the great man now."

Darcy looked up to see Luke Randall walking briskly toward her. Nervously, she turned back toward Sue for support, but all Darcy saw was the back of Sue's white top and navy pants moving rapidly down the hall.

He was wearing a light-yellow shirt and a

brown-and-yellow-striped tie with a dark-brown sweater and brown pants. On his feet he wore the same white Reeboks as yesterday. They were probably more comfortable for doing rounds, Darcy supposed as he approached her.

"Hi," he said good-naturedly. Just as though nothing had happened, she thought with annoyance.

"Good morning," Darcy answered noncommittally.

"I was hoping to see you today." He smiled down warmly at her.

Darn! Those eyes still made her heart do cartwheels. Darcy turned and gazed nonchalantly down the hall.

"I was hoping we could talk a bit about the writing group." He nodded toward the cafeteria at the end of the hall. "Do you have time for a cup of coffee?"

Darcy looked up at him. She didn't really want to talk to him, she decided, but, at the same time, standing there gazing into his eyes and noticing the way they crinkled around the edges when he smiled, she decided that a short talk probably wouldn't do any harm. She glanced casually at her watch. "I suppose so."

"Great!" He put his hand lightly on her arm as they turned and headed toward the cafeteria.

When they entered the large lunchroom,

Darcy was sure every nurse and every aide on the entire staff must be there. Each head seemed to turn, and all eyes were upon them, or so it seemed, as they made their way together down the cafeteria line.

After they were seated at a tiny table over in one corner, he turned and smiled at her. "Listen. About yesterday. . . ."

Darcy looked at him uneasily. "Yes?"

"Well, I want to apologize. I think I may have overreacted."

Their eyes met and locked. "Yes," she said cautiously. "I suppose some might say that."

"Yes, I suppose *some* might." He chuckled. "And am I wrong in suspecting that you might just be one of those *some?*"

Darcy smiled in spite of herself. "I might be," she answered quietly.

He stirred his coffee thoughtfully. "Let me explain something, Ms. Lewis—" He looked tentatively across the table at her. "Uh, Darcy."

Darcy stared down at her coffee. She was surprised at this move into first names, and, although one part of her decided that he had a bit of a nerve, the other part was secretly delighted. She wondered if this first-name use was supposed to go both ways. *Luke,* she imagined herself saying. It was a nice name, but still. . . .

"Now, what I'm about to say—well, please don't take it the wrong way."

Darcy took a deep breath and met his gaze. What was coming up the pike now? she wondered.

"You see, I know you're not trained as a nurse, so there are some things about medical practice that you might not realize."

Darcy took a deep breath. "As a matter of fact," she said steadily, "I was trained as a nurse. In fact, I worked as a nurse for a while. But then I decided to go back to school and get further training. That's when I got my degree in gerontology." She paused. "But you're right. I'm not a practicing nurse—at least not right now." *So, go ahead, make something of it,* she thought belligerently.

He watched her thoughtfully. "I didn't realize that—that you had been a nurse, that is. But what I was going to say was. . . ." He hesitated. "By the way, do you mind if I ask—where did you get your training, as a gerontologist, that is?"

"At St. Monica's College." It was clear from his expression that he had never heard of St. Monica's College. "It's in Chicago—over on the southwest side. It's a small women's college. Well, it was. Actually, there are some guys there now so, officially, at least, it's coed."

"So you have a master's degree in gerontology from this St.. . . ."

"St. Monica's."

"And your degree in nursing?"

"It's from the University of Illinois."

"I see." He was thoughtful for a moment. "So how did you get from nursing into gerontology?"

Darcy leaned back in her chair. She hadn't planned on telling him her whole life story, and especially she hadn't planned to tell him about Grandma. But it was hard to talk about her career change without also mentioning Grandma.

"St. Monica's has a graduate program in gerontology," she said cautiously. "It includes a year of coursework and a year of supervision, out in the field. When you successfully complete the program, you get an MA, and that qualifies you to work with the elderly in a number of different capacities." She paused. "I chose to work both in a retirement home and in a nursing home."

He nodded. "Very interesting. Many people wouldn't choose that, particularly the nursing-home work. It was an interesting choice on your part."

"Yes. Well, I happen to like it a lot." She hesitated. "I like the residents and then, well, there's a personal reason too."

He was silent for a moment, apparently waiting for her to go on. But she decided to leave it at that. She considered her grandmother's illness to be a highly personal matter and, besides, sometimes just talking about Grandma would begin to get to her. And if there was one thing she didn't want, it was to start breaking down in front of Luke Randall, of all people.

"So, anyway, to answer your questions, yes, I am a nurse, and, yes, I do have graduate training in gerontology." She pursed her lips and looked squarely at him. *So go ahead and make a big deal out of that if you want to,* she thought testily.

But he nodded quietly and said nothing.

"So," she said, trying to bring the conversation back to where they had left off, "you were talking about how I should understand more about medical practices or something like that."

He seemed a bit startled. He had been sitting there, looking at her, gazing at her, almost, and then suddenly he looked away, shifting his position as he cleared his throat. "Yes. Well, as you know, in medicine we have to bear in mind the whole patient."

Darcy nodded. "I couldn't agree more."

"And that means that just because there are things that a patient might do that could be fun or interesting, it doesn't mean that that activity is necessarily in the patient's best interest."

"I understand that," Darcy said quietly.

"So even though it was clear that many of the

participants in your writing group yesterday were having a fine time and enjoying themselves, there was also some real tension being created."

Darcy watched him silently.

"Take Louise Ryan, for example."

She just knew this was coming, Darcy told herself.

"Now, the day before, when I had visited Mrs. Ryan, she had been upset and even weeping."

"I know," Darcy said quietly. "Sue Gates told me all about it."

"Then yesterday, when I came into your writing group—even before Wadsworth Logan finished reading about his dog, I was paying particular attention to Mrs. Ryan. Because of what had happened the day before, you understand."

Darcy nodded.

"And I saw Louise Ryan begin to choke up—very early into the story, in fact. I sat there watching her, and even before Wadsworth Logan was finished, she was definitely having a strong emotional reaction. Too strong, in my opinion." He sighed. "I'm sorry, but the whole thing was just creating more stress for the patients than was in their best interest." He looked across at her. "Surely there are other activities that you can do in small groups without creating so much strain on everyone."

"And what would you suggest?" Darcy asked

evenly. "Some embroidery for the ladies, maybe? And perhaps some soap whittling or wood carving for the men?"

He looked at her for a moment without speaking. "I can see that we don't exactly agree," he said finally.

Darcy sighed and leaned back in her chair. "I know I shouldn't question your orders, but the fact is that most of the members of the writing group are not really all that disabled. Oh, I understand that several of them have had strokes, and I don't mean to minimize that. And many of them are frail. But their minds—they're all alert, and they really want to continue to grow. They like being creative, and they seem to love sharing their written thoughts and memories with one another."

"That's fine. But do all these things that they write have to be so sad?" A hint of exasperation was creeping into his voice. "So depressing? Surely the patients can write about things other than losing their families or having their favorite dogs drown!"

"But that's what they *want* to write about!" Darcy looked at him and then sighed in frustration. "After all, I can't censor their writings. I can't tell them, 'Now, folks, be sure you write only about happy, upbeat things.' That's not what all their memories are about." She hesitated. "In fact, that's not even what life is about," she added quietly.

He was silent for a moment. "I'm sorry. I had hoped we could reach an understanding about this." He smiled good-naturedly. "I really had. But I can't have you upsetting the residents this way." He sighed. "Until you have found a way of keeping the material that's brought into the writing group down to a more manageable, less stressful level, we have no choice but to continue to put the whole project on hold."

He glanced at his watch. Darcy could see tiny black hairs clinging to the side of his watchband. She looked away quickly. *Darn!* she thought. *This guy is just too attractive for his own good.*

"I'm going to have to leave. I have rounds back at the hospital at two. I certainly had hoped we could resolve this. But it looks like that's going to have to wait."

He stood up, pulling himself to his full, six-foot height. The way those shoulders and arms filled his brown pullover. . . . Darcy looked away. It was absolutely ridiculous for her to sit here mooning over him, she told herself sternly, when he was practically moving heaven and earth to cancel the project she had worked so hard to develop.

He smiled down at her. "Look. I'm sorry. I really am. But I have to do what I think is best for the patients."

Darcy looked up at him and into his eyes. "I know you do," she said, glancing away. "But I sure wish you had given the writing group a bit more time. I wish you had waited before canceling it. The residents really like the group." She sighed. "Maybe, with time, you would have felt different."

He was silent for a moment. "Tell you what. Let me give it a bit more thought. Maybe we can work out a compromise." He smiled down at her. "Could we talk about it tomorrow? I'll be over at Good Shepherd in the morning. Perhaps we could talk before lunch?"

She nodded briefly and then, after he had said good-bye, she watched as he carried his tray over to the far end of the lunchroom and set it on the counter where all the lunch dishes were stacked.

He sure wasn't easy to work with, she thought as she stood up. She glanced across the room and watched his retreating back as he went out the far door. But he did have a way about him. She picked up her tray and started across the now nearly empty lunchroom. Luke Randall. There was one man, she thought as she placed her tray on the counter, who certainly wasn't going to be easy to forget.

*   *   *

On Friday evening Sue Gates and Darcy sat out on Darcy's front porch, watching the late-August sun set at the far end of the gold fields that stretched lazily out beyond the old farmhouse. They had just finished one of Darcy's famous vegetable-and-cheese casseroles and were leisurely enjoying coffee along with some fresh chocolate-chip cookies that Sue had brought.

"He could have at least called," Sue said as she munched thoughtfully on a cookie.

Darcy nodded. "Right. Because now I don't know whether it's okay to resume the writing group, at least in some kind of modified form, or whether I'm just supposed to wait until he gets around to making up his mind."

"How's it going over at Good Shepherd? Any problems there?"

"No. Fidella Ross is just taking the attitude that until or unless he tells her to stop the group, it's business as usual." Darcy sighed. "Thank heaven for that, anyway. That group is sailing right along. One participant has even started a novel. How about that!"

"Terrific!" Sue paused. "I have an idea, at least, about what may be taking him so long to call. Because I heard there was some sort of crisis at St. Elizabeth Hospital on Wednesday—something to do with the new administration that's coming in there. The whole thing may have peaked soon after he left Towering Oaks on Wednesday. Anyway, he canceled rounds with us for the next two days. And I guess he did the same over at Good Shep. But I still wish he'd found time just to call or leave a message or something. I know he's probably busy, but still, the way it is, we're all left high and dry, not knowing what to do."

Darcy took a sip of coffee. "Some of the residents seem really disappointed too." Across the fields, the sun had turned into a bright-red ball as it sank closer to the distant horizon.

"Tell me about it," Sue said dryly. "Henry Van Dusen—you know how grumpy he can be sometimes."

Darcy grinned. "Do I ever!"

"Well, he was really ticked off. Called Dr. Randall a 'young whippersnapper.' Said he didn't know 'what the blazes he was doing.'"

Darcy giggled delightedly.

"But I just told him, 'Don't worry, Mr. Van Dusen. We'll have that group going again, no matter what.'" She poured herself another cup of coffee. "And then there was Louise Ryan and Wadsworth Logan. Those two were so disappointed."

Darcy nodded. "I know. Incidentally, they've been spending a lot of time together lately, haven't they?"

"Sure have." Sue stretched her long blue-jeaned legs out in front of her and rested them on a nearby stool. "It's really nice. With Wadsworth confined to the wheelchair that way, Louise walks along beside him wherever he goes. They go out to the terrace a lot, where they sit by the hour, just talking."

Darcy sighed. "That's neat."

"It really is," Sue agreed. "They've become great friends. You know, Louise isn't really particularly ill. I mean, it's not like she's had a stroke, like Wadsworth. In fact, the main reason she's at Towering Oaks is that she's so frail. Her bones simply aren't what they used to be, and she and her son both felt that she couldn't manage alone anymore."

Out to the west, the blazing red ball was sinking down behind the field. "Look at that," Sue said, nodding toward the setting sun. "Isn't that beautiful!"

They were silent a moment as they watched the sun slowly disappear behind the distant prairie. The sun seemed particularly red tonight, with rays that lingered for a remarkably long time, and its stunning beauty made Darcy think longingly of her grandmother. *How Grandma would have loved it,* she thought.

"I'm glad Louise Ryan and Wadsworth Logan have found each other," she said finally. "Even if it is late in life—it's nice that they have developed such a warm, caring relationship."

"Oh, it's never too late." Sue laughed. "Who knows? Maybe there's still hope for you and me. Well, of *course* there's hope for you," she said, smiling as she corrected herself. "You're still young. What are you now? Twenty-five?"

"Twenty-six," Darcy corrected her. "Twenty-seven in January."

"Okay. So you're twenty-six—going on twenty-seven. You've still got loads of time to find someone nice, settle down, and all that."

"Right," Darcy said sardonically. "*Loads* of time."

"But me," Sue went on, pointedly ignoring Darcy's caustic comment, "well, seeing Louise Ryan and Wadsworth Logan, who knows? Maybe there is hope for me, after all."

"Oh, Sue, don't be ridiculous! Of course there's 'hope,' as you call it. You make yourself sound like you're about ninety-nine. Honestly! People your age get remarried all the time."

"Fifty-two, Darcy, as of last May twentieth." She pulled her legs off the stool and put them squarely on the floor as she turned to face Darcy. "Do you realize how few women my age ever find anyone again?" She sighed and leaned back in her chair. "Chances are something like one in ten."

"So, you may well be one of those one in ten.

After all, fifty-two or not, you're still a knock-out."

Sue pushed her short, curly hair away from her forehead. "Don't be ridiculous. My hair is going gray, and my face is covered with wrinkles." She ran one hand tentatively along her chin.

"Covered with wrinkles! Oh, spare me! Sue, honestly, I don't know what you see when you look in the mirror. But whatever it is, it's certainly not what other people see. You are *not* covered with wrinkles. Your skin is mature—"

"Right," Sue said grimly. "Mature."

"By that I merely mean that you don't look seventeen. Neither do I. But you've got great skin. And your hair is gorgeous. That gray looks like highlights, for heaven's sake. Why, people in Chicago pay hundreds of dollars to get silvery highlights like that put in their hair!"

"Well, people in Chicago must be crazy, then," Sue muttered.

Darcy looked out across the field. Only a few rays remained from the setting sun. She and Sue had had this same conversation countless times, she thought. And, without fail, Sue always got off on this kick about how old she thought she looked, and Darcy, in frustration, always came back with how, regardless of her age, Sue was still slim and gorgeous.

But it was a losing battle. Periodically Sue got

demoralized about her age. It probably wouldn't have been so bad, Darcy thought, if Rich had lived. Then Sue would have had someone to love her and give her the caring, positive feedback she deserved. It had been tough for Sue, being alone all these years.

Sue's husband had been killed in Vietnam the year after he and Sue were married. An officer in the regular Army, he had gone to Vietnam on his third combat mission. It was to have been his last. Sue had never really recovered from the loss. In fact, it was only recently that she had even hinted that she could get interested in another relationship. Darcy had been happy to hear that. But still, she wished Sue wouldn't worry so much about her age.

"I suppose you think I worry too much about my age," Sue said, interrupting the silence.

Darcy looked at her in surprise. "As a matter of fact, I was just thinking that."

"I know. And you're probably wondering if you'll be this hung up on age when you're fifty-two."

Darcy nodded. "As a matter of fact. . . ."

"And you think you never will be."

"That's right. I don't think I will be."

"Right. That's what I thought, too, when I was twenty-six."

They looked at each other, and both burst out

laughing together. "Honestly," Darcy said as she wiped tears of laughter from her face, "we ought to just make a record of this conversation and then simply put it on and listen to it every couple of weeks. That would save us all the hassle of going through it again and again."

"Right!" Sue said, still laughing. "After all, we each know by now what the other's going to say."

"And how!" And they were silent for a moment as they sat contentedly watching the lightning bugs across the distant fields.

"You're finally getting over Rich, aren't you?" Darcy said quietly as she turned toward her friend.

Sue nodded. "Yes. I really am. I still miss him, of course. I always will. But, yes, I think I'm finally over him." She was quiet for a moment. "I even think I could fall in love again now. In fact, I know I could. If the right man came along. . . ." She turned toward Darcy. "What about you? Are you still carrying the torch for Douglas? Or do you think—"

Darcy sighed. "Oh, I don't know, Sue. Yes. I guess I'm pretty much over him by now." She was thoughtful for a moment, remembering Douglas and their years together downstate at the University of Illinois.

Douglas had been a business major, and they had met during their sophomore year. They had fallen in love almost at once. After graduation, they had continued to date, gotten engaged, even.

And then one day, not long after Darcy's grandmother had started showing signs of some serious mental deterioration, Douglas had simply announced that he had been offered a great new job in Southern California. He wanted Darcy to come with him, get married, and together they'd buy a big house in Orange County, he said, with a swimming pool, no less.

But Darcy had told him that she couldn't go, that she couldn't just abandon her grandmother that way, and all he had said was that that was too bad. This job, he had told her, was a once-in-a-lifetime opportunity. It would really put him in the fast lane, and it was altogether too good to even think of turning down.

The next thing Darcy knew, he was gone. A year later she heard that he had gotten married and was indeed living in Orange County with a big house, a beautiful wife, and a swimming pool. He got everything he ever wanted, she thought bitterly.

Abruptly Darcy brought herself back to the present.

"You've just got to start looking around," Sue was saying. "Be a little more open to meeting men. For someone your age there are still plenty of them out there." She was quiet for a moment.

"You'll meet someone, someone nice. I can just feel it." She reached over and squeezed Darcy's hand. "You wait and see. And now"—she stood up and stretched—"I've got to be getting on home. After all, I'm on at seven in the morning."

Darcy glanced at her watch and was surprised to see that it was almost ten. She stood up and began gathering the coffee cups. "I didn't know it was so late, either."

"It's been great, as usual," Sue said as she stood by the kitchen door. "Your casserole was spectacular, as always." She reached out and gave Darcy a quick hug. "Thanks a million."

Darcy smiled back happily at her. "My pleasure. And remember," she called out the door as Sue made her way across the yard and toward her car, "when you look in the mirror tonight, those so-called wrinkles are *not* on your face; they're in your mind!"

Sue waved back. "And you remember—that Douglas was a creep. A first-class jerk. Didn't know what he was giving up. Forget him, Darcy." She opened the car door. "Think about the future. Something great's going to happen! You wait and see."

"For both of us," Darcy called back. "*You* wait and see."

"Got my fingers crossed!" And Sue closed the car door and started the motor. Then, leaning across the front seat, she rolled down the window on the passenger side. "And remember—think positive!"

Darcy nodded. "I will if you will."

"It's a deal!" Sue gave a final wave, rolled up the window, and drove away.

Darcy stood in front of the bathroom mirror in her pajamas and terry-cloth robe, carefully putting night cream on her face. When she was through, she reached for her brush and began lightly brushing her light-brown, shoulder-length hair.

"A hundred strokes a night, just before you go to bed," Grandma used to tell her. "It's good for the scalp and makes the hair shine."

Darcy knew now that the hundred-strokes-a-night routine was probably not one of Grandma's greatest ideas. Today most experts agreed that ten or twenty strokes were plenty. But even so, she still liked to brush her hair just before she went to bed.

She put the brush down and leaned closer to the mirror. The light-gray eyes that looked back at her were clear and bright, and her hair shone in the reflected bathroom light. Maybe Grandma was right, after all, she thought with a smile as she put down her brush and headed toward bed.

After she turned off the light, Darcy lay for a

while thinking about the evening and her conversation with Sue. Yes, she decided, she really was over the whole thing with Douglas, and, as Sue had taken pains to point out, the guy really was a first-class jerk. Not worth losing any more sleep over, she told herself, and she turned comfortably to one side.

But it *would* be nice to meet someone else, she thought dreamily as she began to drift off to sleep. Someone kind and gentle and thoughtful. Someone who would really love her, not someone like Douglas who never really cared at all. No, Darcy thought, she'd like to meet someone new and completely different. She wondered lazily what he would look like. Tall, she thought. And nice looking. He didn't have to be heart-stopping gorgeous, of course—just nice looking would do.

She began to drift off. He'd look like—let's see, she thought. Dreamily a face began to emerge in her half-asleep, half-awake state. That's what he would look like. That would be nice, she thought lazily from what seemed far, far away.

Darcy sat bolt upright in bed. Luke! That was who she had been thinking about. Luke Randall!

With a groan Darcy fell back on the bed. *Oh, no!* she thought. *Not him. He's such a pain in the neck sometimes.* But still, she thought as she began once more to drift dreamily off to sleep, he sure was handsome.

Chapter Four

Mondays were always important days at Good Shepherd. On Monday morning staff members from the Littlefield County Animal Shelter visited the nursing home, bringing with them four or five well-behaved, friendly dogs and several older, quiet, and serene cats. The residents loved having the animals visit, and the project's huge success had caused Darcy to view this as one of her most successful innovations. It was good for the animals, and it brightened the whole week for the residents.

The Animal Shelter's blue-and-white van was already in the Good Shepherd parking lot when Darcy pulled in on Monday morning. *Good,* she thought as she got out of her car and started across the lot. She was glad Pete Hiller, the shelter's administrator, had gotten an early start.

And she was certainly relieved, she told herself as she glanced nonchalantly around the lot, not to find Luke Randall's sleek gray Thunderbird parked there. Throughout the weekend that man had been hovering somewhere around the background of her thoughts, and she was definitely glad that Monday finally had come. Now, perhaps, she could get him off her mind and put her attention back to serious business again.

It was ridiculous for her to be thinking about him, of all people, she told herself as she opened the side door and started down the hall. After all, ever since she had first met him, Luke Randall had brought her nothing but trouble. She certainly did not need anyone like him in her life, she reminded herself for the hundredth time since Friday. No way.

The dayroom bubbled with excitement. Roy Bogan, who had recently turned one hundred, sat in his wheelchair, his bony hands gently petting a plump, contented cat that sat blissfully purring, eyes closed, cuddled in his lap. Darcy went over and put one hand on Roy's frail shoulder.

"Good morning, Mr. Bogan," she said cheerfully.

"Oh, hello, Darcy," he said, looking up.

"What a beautiful cat!" Darcy reached down to stroke the soft fur.

"Her name is Twinkles. And she's been sitting right here, right on my lap, ever since Pete Hiller got here this morning. Hasn't moved once."

"I guess Twinkles must really like you, Mr. Bogan."

Roy chuckled. "She's a good cat, Darcy. Re-

minds me of a cat I had as a boy." And contentedly he returned to petting Twinkles.

At the other end of the room, Pete Hiller was
showing a delighted group of residents how a
beautiful collie named Laddie would sit, fetch, lie
down, and heel on command.

"Hi, Darcy." Pete waved as Darcy approached
the little group.

"Darcy, you should see this dog," one of the
residents called out happily. "He is just amaz-
ing."

The other members of the little group nodded
in agreement. "So well trained," someone said.
"Wonderful disposition," another added. "So in-
telligent."

Darcy pulled up a chair and sat watching as
Laddie and Pete Hiller continued the routine.
Along one side of the table, Cordelia Campanella, who was ninety-one and made her way
around the halls of Good Shepherd with the help
of a walker, began to sneeze. Darcy found a box
of tissues on a nearby shelf and took them over
to her.

"Thank you, dear," Cordelia said, wiping her
nose. "The animals always make me sneeze a little—an old allergy of mine, you know." She
smiled up at Darcy. "But I don't mind. I always
enjoy them so much, especially the dogs." And
she leaned back in her chair, gently wiping her

eyes as she continued to watch Laddie going through his paces.

Coming down the corridor, Darcy saw Fidella Ross slowly pushing a familiar figure in a wheelchair. Darcy jumped to her feet and started up the hall to meet her. "Hi, Grandma," she called out as she waved happily at the tiny figure bundled up in a blanket and huddled in the oversized chair.

"Your grandmother thought she'd like to come down and visit with our friends from the animal shelter," Fidella said cheerfully as Darcy approached.

"Great idea!" Darcy bent down and kissed the small, withered cheek.

Grandma beamed up at her. "Hello, Nurse," she said in her frail, scratchy voice.

"No, Priscilla," Fidella said gently. "That's Darcy, your granddaughter. Remember Darcy?"

Grandma nodded, but it was clear that she didn't know what Fidella meant. Fidella looked at Darcy and shook her head sympathetically.

Meanwhile, Grandma's attention had wandered on to the dayroom. To the delight of a growing group of admirers, Laddie and Pete Hiller were continuing with Laddie's obedience routine. Several of the residents were now applauding enthusiastically as Laddie's repertoire expanded.

"Char-lee," Grandma said as she pointed toward the well-trained collie.

Darcy watched, confused. From what she had heard over the years, she had always thought that the legendary Charlie had been a much smaller dog, more the size of a dachshund or maybe even a little terrier. But Grandma continued to point and laugh delightedly as Fidella wheeled her over to the group, which, with rapt attention, was still watching Laddie and Pete Hiller.

Pete Hiller turned and walked across the room to where Roy Bogan sat, still holding the contented Twinkles in his lap. Pete turned and faced Laddie, who sat upright as he attentively watched Pete from the other side of the room. Fidella quietly wheeled Grandma's chair over next to Roy Bogan's.

"Laddie, come!" Pete called firmly, and without a second's hesitation Laddie stood up and trotted happily across the floor. The residents applauded in delight. When Laddie got in front of Pete, he sat down on his haunches and gazed intently up at him.

"Good boy." Pete reached out and gently scratched Laddie's ear. "Now, down," he commanded, and immediately Laddie dropped to the floor, his front legs stretched out in front of him. "Good boy," Pete said as he patted Laddie affectionately. "Very good boy."

"Char-lee," Grandma said from beside Roy. She pointed happily toward Laddie. "Char-lee."

Darcy sat down cross-legged on the floor, positioning herself between Laddie and Grandma's wheelchair. "Grandma, this dog's name is Laddie." Darcy reached out and began petting Laddie's soft coat. "Isn't he a nice dog, Grandma?"

Grandma smiled delightedly. "Smart," she said, giving a soft little chuckle.

"He certainly is, Grandma."

"How do you like this cat, Priscilla?" Roy interjected as he turned to face Darcy's grandmother. "Her name is Twinkles."

"Oh—pretty," Grandma said as she briefly turned her attention toward Roy and Twinkles. "But that's Charlie. . . ." She looked back at Laddie and then at Darcy. "Did you feed Charlie, Laura?"

"That's Darcy," Roy said a bit impatiently. "Her name is Darcy, Priscilla, not Laura. You're getting your granddaughter mixed up with someone else."

But Grandma ignored Roy's comment and went on smiling at Darcy. "Don't forget to feed Charlie, Laura. He's a good dog."

Darcy sighed. "No, Grandma, I won't."

"That's too bad, Darcy," Roy said, looking over at Darcy. "Your grandmother just can't seem to remember your name anymore."

Darcy nodded. "I know," she said quietly. She looked at her grandmother, still happily watching Laddie. "But there's nothing she can do about it. It's not her fault."

With the help of her walker, Cordelia came over and joined the little group. One of the aides helped her sit down in a nearby chair. "Why can't your grandmother remember your"—Cordelia stopped and reached for a nearby tissue—"your name, Darcy?" she asked after a hearty sneeze.

"My grandmother has Alzheimer's disease, Mrs. Campanella," Darcy said quietly.

Ever since she had entered gerontology, Darcy had made it a point to be as honest as she could with the residents. If one patient was genuinely concerned about another, Darcy felt that, barring unusual circumstances, it was best to be as truthful as possible. Otherwise, she believed, she would be treating the residents as though they were children.

"Is that what they call being senile?" Cordelia asked.

Darcy nodded. "Sort of. Or at least that's what they used to call it. But that was back in the days when they thought that—sooner or later—all of us, as we got older, would get a bit senile. And now we know that isn't really true. Most older people don't get senile."

"That's good," Cordelia said quietly. "You know, I always worry a bit about that—such as when my children or grandchildren come to visit. Sometimes I get their names mixed up. Especially the little ones. There are so many of them now, you know—eight grandchildren and twelve great-grandchildren. Anyway, sometimes I wonder if they're looking at me and thinking, 'Oh, listen to Grandma—she sounds so foolish.' " She was thoughtful for a moment. "I worry about that sometimes."

Darcy reached out and squeezed her hand. "Well, don't. You're a sharp lady—not a bit like my grandmother. You see, what they used to call senility, they now know is really some kind of a brain disorder. The most frequent brain disorder is Alzheimer's disease, which causes the brain not to work right, not to transmit signals correctly. And then sometimes those same symptoms can be caused by tiny strokes—brain infarctions, they call them. That's what they mean by 'related disorders.' It's basically the same set of symptoms but with a different cause. But with my grandmother, it's just plain Alzheimer's, which has destroyed a number of her brain cells."

Cordelia turned and sadly watched Darcy's grandmother, whose frail body was hunched over in her wheelchair as she went on talking meaninglessly to Laddie and Pete Hiller. "That's really too bad, Darcy," Cordelia said quietly. "I never quite understood that before. Sometimes when I see the patients from that wing"—she nodded toward the ARD section—"I wonder if it's just a matter of time before I'm up there myself, babbling away."

"No, Mrs. Campanella, I don't think so. You seem mentally as fit as a fiddle to me. And look at Mr. Bogan here. . . ."

Roy Bogan looked up from Twinkles, who was contentedly sleeping in his lap.

"One hundred years old," Darcy said, "and sharp as they come."

Roy chuckled. "Oh, I do the best I can, Darcy. Try to keep my mind active, you know. By the way, I just finished reading one of those books that you brought into the library—it was another western by that young fellow, Louis L'Amour. I really love those books!"

"Terrific!" Darcy said. By soliciting donations from interested persons in the community, Darcy had been able to build up a small library of lively, readable books at Good Shepherd. The library had become one of her favorite projects since joining the staff, and she was always glad to hear that the books were being read and enjoyed.

She pulled herself to her feet. "So how about joining the writing group, Mr. Bogan? We're going to meet again tomorrow morning at nine o'clock. Maybe you could start writing a western of your own. How about it?"

Roy looked up at her quizzically. "You know, I was thinking about something like that. I think I'd sort of like that. I've got to admit I have been thinking about a couple of ideas for a western. But then, I'm the oldest one here. One hundred years old. You don't think the others would say—"

"They'd say 'fantastic and more power to you.'" Darcy rested her hand lightly on his shoulder. "Honestly, we'd be delighted to have you. How about it?"

Roy smiled up at her delightedly. "Well, I'll give it some thought. I've read so much of that Louis L'Amour. I wonder—if I just put my mind to it, maybe I could do something like that too."

"It's worth a shot. You never know."

Roy chuckled. "Not unless you try, you don't."

"Right. So you'll be there tomorrow morning?"

He nodded emphatically. "You can count on it."

"Great!" Darcy said, then she turned to circulate around the room. Over on the other side, one of Pete's assistants was demonstrating the skills of a beautiful, well-behaved golden retriever to an enthusiastic group of admirers. Nearby, another aide was showing a basket with a mother cat and a litter of tiny kittens to a group of delighted residents.

Darcy bent down to gently kiss her grandmother, who, with rapt attention, was still gazing at Laddie, and she then turned toward the other end of the dayroom.

"You certainly have generated quite a lot of activity around here today," a voice behind her said softly.

"Oh!" Darcy whirled around and looked directly into the warm brown eyes of Luke Randall. "I didn't know you were—"

"That I was here?" He smiled down at her. "Yes. I'm here. Have been for the last five minutes or so. I was over there, by the door, talking with Fidella Ross."

Darcy looked quickly over toward the door that led to the main corridor. As their eyes met, Fidella shrugged noncommittally, as if to say what else could she do.

"So, I understand that today is animal-shelter day."

Darcy cleared her throat. "Yes. As a matter of fact, every Monday—"

"I know. Fidella told me. Every Monday some dogs and cats are brought into the nursing home."

"Yes. The patients just love them, you know,"

Darcy said, feeling suddenly defensive. "After all, research does show that—"

"That holding or talking with a pet often improves elderly persons' morale, their sense of well-being, and it can also lower blood pressure." He paused and looked down at her. "I know all that. But I also note that here, at least, it has also activated one patient's allergy." He nodded toward Cordelia Campanella, who was still sneezing with regularity. "And though I don't want to be a killjoy, there is one dog over there"—he nodded toward the far corner of the room where a small dog had begun barking insistently at the mother cat—"that is making a fair amount of noise. Some of the patients who aren't in the dayroom, who might not be feeling so well, could be a bit bothered by all the noise, you know."

"That's probably true," Darcy said, looking around nervously. "Perhaps I just ought to go over there and see what I can do to quiet down the dog that's doing all the barking."

Luke nodded toward Cordelia. "And I'll go over and see what, if anything, I can do about this lady's allergy."

Darn! Darcy thought as she crossed the room. *Why did he have to be here this morning? Now he's probably going to raise a big fuss and complain that the animals cause allergies or that the dogs make too much noise.*

But by the time she reached the other end of the room, the dog that had been causing the disturbance had settled down and was happily resting in one of the patients' laps. Meanwhile, the mother cat was blissfully feeding her babies to the continued delight of the small group of residents who had gathered around to watch.

Darcy stood and chatted with the group for a few minutes, but out of one corner of her eye, she stole an occasional glance at Luke. He was sitting now and apparently talking with the little group that had gathered around Laddie. *He's probably trying to find out from Mrs. Campanella just how bad her allergy is,* Darcy thought. She was glad that Cordelia had vigorously maintained that watching the animals was definitely worth the sneezing bout. At least it wouldn't sound as though Darcy were deliberately inflicting pain or discomfort on the patients.

After a while she left the group with the mother cat and strolled casually across the busy room toward the group that was clustered around Laddie. As she approached, she could see that Luke was talking earnestly with one of the patients. He probably was still discussing Cordelia's allergy with her, Darcy thought impatiently.

But as she approached, she saw that Luke wasn't talking with Cordelia at all. In fact, he wasn't even near her. Instead, he was sitting next to Roy, and he was leaning forward, talking intently with one of the patients in a wheelchair.

Darcy quickened her step. It couldn't be. . . . But as she got closer, she realized that it was. Luke was talking to Grandma. Or, to be more exact, he was listening to Grandma. There he was, leaning forward, elbows resting on his knees and gently holding one of Grandma's tiny, bony hands in each of his as he listened intently to every word she said.

Grandma was telling him about Grandpa. Even though Grandpa had been dead for more than twenty-five years, Grandma was talking about him as though he had just stepped out a minute ago.

"Yes," she was saying in her frail, thin voice, "Hank went out to feed the chickens. But he'll be back in a little while."

"And how about you?" Luke asked gently. "How are things going for you?"

"Oh, just fine, fine." She glanced up and saw Darcy. "There's Laura," she said, smiling delightedly.

Luke turned and looked up at Darcy. "Laura?" he asked, surprised.

"Laura was my mother's name," Darcy said softly.

Luke furrowed his brow. "Oh."

Beside him, Roy, who was still petting the contented Twinkles as he listened in on the conversation, leaned forward in his chair. "Darcy's Priscilla's granddaughter, Doc. But Priscilla can't ever get it straight." He sighed impatiently. "One minute she calls Darcy 'Laura,' the next minute it's 'Nurse,' and the next it's something else." He leaned back in his chair. "Priscilla's memory is terrible." He shook his head. "I hope mine never gets that bad."

Luke looked at Darcy. "I didn't realize. . . ." He turned and glanced at Grandma. "This lady is your grandmother?" he asked, looking once more at Darcy.

Darcy nodded. "That's right." She pulled a stool over and perched next to Grandma's wheelchair. "I owe everything in the world to her." She paused as she studied her grandmother's frail features. "She gave me all that anyone could want. I loved her so much," she added softly. And then she caught herself. "And, of course, I still do—love her, that is."

Luke reached out and put his hand over Darcy's. His grasp felt warm and gentle. "You don't have to apologize. I understand. Honestly, I do. You were more nearly right the first time. The person you knew and loved, *really* loved, that is, isn't even here anymore, is she?"

Darcy looked down and slowly shook her

head. Luke was the first person who had ever really said it, who had ever actually put into words the feelings of grief that had, at times, so overwhelmed her. Because he was right. The Grandma whom Darcy had loved, grown up with, laughed with—that Grandma was gone, and a strange, frail, little person had taken her place. And yet, at the same time, this tiny person also was Grandma. It didn't make sense.

Darcy reached across the table for one of Cordelia's tissues. It was embarrassing to have her eyes fill up this way, right here on the job. But no one had ever expressed it like that before; no one else had ever understood.

She dabbed gently at her eyes and looked at Luke. "That's right," she said softly. "Grandma's here, but—"

"But she isn't."

Darcy nodded.

Luke squeezed her hand. "It's one of the toughest losses there is." He looked back at Grandma, who was chuckling with delight over Laddie. "But remember, as far as anyone can tell, it's the survivors—people like you—who feel the loss the most. The actual victims of the disease, like your grandmother, don't seem to suffer nearly so much. At least, not the way the family does."

He let go of Darcy's hand and turned back toward Grandma. But by now Grandma was absorbed in watching Pete and Laddie go through some more obedience paces. Luke reached out and gently touched Grandma's hand. But when there was no response, he nodded toward the hall, indicating to Darcy that they could talk better out there.

"I think I know what you're going through," he said when they were safely out in the hall. "And it's tough."

Darcy nodded, still trying to hold back the tears.

He glanced at his watch. "I have to make rounds. But I'd like to talk with you more about this." He lowered his voice. "Alzheimer's is very hard to deal with. Maybe I could help."

Darcy looked at him quizzically.

"Since entering geriatrics, I've seen a lot of Alzheimer's patients, and I have some idea of the strain it brings on family members. Who knows? Maybe just talking it over might make it a bit easier for you. Look, would it be okay if I gave you a call?"

"That would be—uh, fine," Darcy said hesitantly, suddenly recalling the last call she had had from him, about the writing group at Towering Oaks. She didn't want another call like that one. But then, there didn't seem too much chance of that now.

"Great. I'll talk with you later." And he was gone, walking briskly down the hall toward one of the wards.

"I don't believe it!" Sue Gates said incredulously when Darcy arrived at Towering Oaks that afternoon. "What did he mean he'd call you? Call you where? Here? At home? Is he going to ask you out? What's going on?"

"Sue! Don't be so hyper! I don't *know*. The man didn't say. All he said was, 'Look, I'll call you.' He said he'd like to talk with me some more about Grandma. But, no, he didn't say, 'Let's go out, let's go to a show, let's have dinner.' Nothing like that."

"But still, it sounds that way." Sue smiled. "Oh, I know he's a pain in the neck sometimes, but he is *so* handsome!"

Darcy smiled back at her mischievously. "Yes. I've noticed that myself."

A buzzer rang from down the hall, and Sue stood up to answer it. "Well, it sure is interesting, anyway." She started down the hall. "Keep me posted."

"Will do," Darcy said as she stepped behind the nurses' station to check through the morning's notes.

Since nothing significant had happened since yesterday, Darcy began to make preparations for that afternoon's discussion group. One day a week several of the residents at Towering Oaks gathered to discuss a book or a short story that they had chosen to read. It was a lively group and another of Darcy's innovations that the participants seemed to enjoy and look forward to.

"Excuse me."

Darcy looked up, startled. A tall, gray-haired man, about fifty, stood at the nurses' station. He was wearing a tweed sports coat, and he carried a slim attaché case. Darcy didn't remember ever seeing him before.

"My name is Zeke Ryan. My mother is a resident here. Louise Ryan."

Darcy nodded. "Oh, of course." It was Louise Ryan who had wept so profusely at Wadsworth Logan's dog story last week. Darcy couldn't remember ever having seen Mrs. Ryan's son before.

"I'd like to see my mother, if I may."

"Yes, of course." Darcy looked around for the visitors' sign-in sheet. "Just a minute. I think I'll have to find Mrs. Gates, the head nurse. She'll arrange for you to have a quiet place to visit with your mother."

He nodded as Darcy turned and headed briskly down the hall. She met Sue as she rounded the first corner and explained to her about Zeke Ryan's unexpected visit.

"I thought Louise Ryan's son was out of the

country," Sue said as they hurried back toward the nurses' station. "She talks about him all the time. She'll be absolutely delighted!"

When they approached the nurses' station, Sue said cheerfully to the distinguished-looking stranger, "Good afternoon. You're Louise Ryan's son?"

"Yes, I am," Zeke Ryan said, smiling warmly.

Their eyes held for a moment, and then Sue said, "And you'd like to visit with her."

"I certainly would. I haven't been able to see my mother for a long time."

Sue looked down at the visitors' registration log. "Yes," she said softly. "Well, I know she'll be delighted to see you. Here, will you sign in, please?" She handed him a sheet on a clipboard and a ballpoint pen.

Without a word he took the pen and scrawled his name on the next available line. *Zeke Ryan,* Darcy saw him write. *Washington, D.C.*

He looked up and handed the pen and the clipboard back to Sue.

"If you'll just come this way," Sue said, stepping out from behind the nurses' station, "I think we can find your mother. She's either in the dayroom or out on the terrace."

And without so much as a look toward Darcy, Sue and Zeke Ryan started briskly down the hall, chatting like old friends.

A quick glance at her watch told Darcy that she'd better get to the seminar room. It was time for the book discussion group to start.

Later that evening Darcy lay staring at the darkened ceiling as she tried unsuccessfully to go to sleep. She was lying in the great four-poster in the upstairs bedroom that had been hers since she was a child. She had been there for more than an hour, hoping that sleep would come. After all, she had to be over at Good Shepherd at eight in the morning, and it was now almost midnight. This would never do, she told herself as she changed her position for the hundredth time. She *had* to get some sleep.

She rolled over on her side and looked out the window. Of course, she could get up and pull down the shade, she reminded herself. The full moon shining in her room certainly wasn't helping any. But for some reason—and she wasn't exactly sure why—she didn't feel much like moving, like getting up and shutting out the moonlight. It was rather nice, just lying here, gazing out the window and seeing the stars, and thinking about . . . well, just thinking about everything.

But mainly she was thinking about Luke and about the call she had had from him during the evening. They had talked for more than an hour, and, during that call Darcy had discovered another side of Luke Randall, a quiet, gentle side that cared about people, that felt genuine concern about suffering, and that wanted to do something about it.

She also had found that he shared her own deep concern for the problems of the elderly. He was undertaking a second residency, this one in geriatrics, he had told her, because he believed that geriatrics was a field of medicine that was too frequently overlooked by young doctors when they chose their field of specialization.

"Many doctors don't have much interest in working with the elderly," he had told her on the phone. "But then, that's not too surprising. So many people still tend to think of older folks as being somehow different—very distant from themselves. They don't seem to realize that growing old is something that we all do, that aging is a normal part of our growth cycle." He paused. "I've got to tell you—sometimes I get really impatient with people who speak of older people as though they were some kind of strange species. We're all the same, you know; it's just that the older folks have been around longer, that's all."

Darcy agreed. She and Sue had discussed this issue many times—over dinner, in the summer evenings out on Darcy's front porch, or over lunch at the Towering Oaks cafeteria. But aside from Sue, Darcy had not found too many other people who really shared these feelings. It was good to find someone like Luke who felt the same way.

So why was she lying here, she asked herself, unable to fall asleep, thinking about Luke? Just because he shared her commitment to the elderly? Did that make him a reason to lie awake and stare out at the moon and spend half the night thinking about him?

It certainly did not, Darcy told herself sternly as she rolled over on her side, away from the window, and pulled her quilt up around her shoulders. No reason at all.

Tomorrow was September first, she thought, her eyelids beginning to feel heavy. Autumn. Her favorite season. She supposed that, like so much else in her life, her particular love for these early fall months came from her grandmother. How Grandma used to love the first signs of autumn! It always reminded her of harvesttime, she would tell Darcy—back when she was growing up on an Illinois prairie farm.

Every year Grandma would delight in that first reddish tinge in the leaves, the freshness of a September morning, the clear, cool breeze that gently danced through the old farmhouse on an early fall night. *Like tonight,* Darcy thought, pulling the comforter closer around her. Behind her, she could hear the bedroom curtains gently rustling in the fresh autumn breeze.

Grandma would have loved a night like this, Darcy thought. But what about Luke? she wondered. Did he like autumn too? She took a slow, deep breath. She hoped so, she thought lazily as sleep began to overtake her. She hoped that he liked autumn, with its blazing trees, fresh crisp apples, frosty mornings, and brisk evenings. She hoped that he liked the autumn harvest as much as she did.

Chapter Five

"**G**uess what!" Sue said when Darcy arrived at Towering Oaks the next afternoon. "Your writing group has been reinstated."

Darcy looked at her in delight. "When did that happen?"

"Just this morning. One of the first things Dr. Randall did when he got here today was to seek out the group's participants. He talked to Helen-Marie Wiggins and Henry Van Dusen and Wadsworth Logan and all the others, but especially he talked for a long time with Louise Ryan."

"And?"

"And I guess he asked them about the group and what they were getting out of it. Because he told me that Louise said that even though she cried when Wadsworth read his dog story, that didn't mean that she was unhappy or sad. She said she just found the story very touching and that she still loved the writing group, looked forward to it, wanted to go on with it, and so on."

"That's terrific!" Darcy said excitedly.

"In fact, I guess everyone he talked to said the

same thing, that they really loved the group and didn't want to see it end. And guess what— Henry actually called Dr. Randall a 'young whippersnapper' right to his face. He told him he ought to listen to you—that he could learn a thing or two that way."

"Oh, no!" Darcy covered her face with her hand. "He didn't!"

Sue grinned. "He sure did."

"I'm almost afraid to ask—but I will, anyway. How did Luke take *that?*"

"Believe it or not, he took it just fine. In fact— and you're going to find this hard to believe—he was the one who told me about it."

"You're kidding."

Sue held up her right hand. "Scout's honor. Dr. Luke Randall was right up here at the nurses' station, chuckling about the whole thing. He actually admitted that he overreacted the other day, said he took all the crying—especially Louise Ryan's—the wrong way. He said that at the time he just thought it was bad for the residents, that they needed something more upbeat. But then when he began to think about it, and especially after he sat down and talked with them today, he realized he was wrong. And what's more, he admitted it! Can you imagine—a doctor who actually admits he's made a mistake!" Sue shook her head in wonder. "You know, I'm beginning to really like this guy. I think he's okay."

Darcy turned toward the hall. "You're right. He really is okay. In fact," she called casually over her shoulder, "he and I had a long talk on the phone last night."

"You *what?* You didn't tell me that."

"You didn't ask!" Darcy waved mischievously over her shoulder as she headed down the hall toward the dayroom.

"I'm glad you agreed to have dinner with me," Luke said on Saturday evening as he switched off the Thunderbird's ignition key and turned to face Darcy. He had picked her up earlier that evening, and they had driven to a lovely French restaurant in one of Chicago's far southwest suburbs. Darcy had not been in that area before, and she thoroughly enjoyed the surroundings and the peaceful ambiance.

At a table overlooking a spacious, immaculately kept golf course, they had enjoyed some excellent clams Bordelaise, and later they lingered over huge mugs of rich, dark coffee as they watched the setting sun. Now, parked in the driveway next to the old farmhouse, they sat side by side, looking out at the moonlit yard.

It certainly wasn't her practice to invite men into the house after a date, and as she watched the tiny light of a faraway jet lazily make its way across the darkened sky, Darcy considered whether she should make an exception for Luke. Maybe it would be all right, she told herself. He seemed such a gentleman.

"If you invited me in for coffee," he said, interrupting her thoughts, "I wouldn't turn you down."

Darcy laughed. "You know, I was just about to do that."

He smiled warmly. "Well, I think you should." He turned and opened the car door and jumped out. A moment later he was opening the passenger door and holding her hand as she stepped out.

She stood beside him, her head barely reaching his shoulder, and looked across the prairie that stretched out in front of the farmhouse. "You see," she said softly, "this is why I love it here so much." Her hand was still resting lightly in his, and neither made a move to change it. "The prairie and fields—that's why I haven't moved in closer to the city." She looked up at the old house, its form clearly outlined in the moonlight. "I've lived in this house most of my life. This is home."

He looked at the house and back across the fields. Then, dropping her hand, he put one arm lightly around her shoulders. His touch was gentle but firm, and, almost without thinking, Darcy let her head rest lightly against his shoulder.

They stood like that for several minutes, gazing out across the moonlit prairie, and then he took a step sideways and put both hands on her shoulders, turning her gently toward him.

"You have a lovely place here. And, furthermore, you are very lovely too." He bent down and kissed her lightly on the forehead. His kiss was warm and gentle, and somewhere deep inside her Darcy felt a tiny stir, like little cartwheels.

"Well," she said briskly, trying to bring herself back to reality, "we were talking about having some coffee."

He smiled down at her. "Right."

In the kitchen, she measured coffee beans and dumped them into the grinder. One, two, three, four, five. . . . Or was the last spoonful only four? She stood and gazed at the grinder's receptacle, trying to assess its contents. She was pretty sure she had put in five. Darn! What kind of coffee would she turn out if she hadn't even measured the beans right!

Behind her, Luke sat at the kitchen table, and she could feel him idly watching her. With exaggerated nonchalance she dumped the beans into a cup and began measuring again. One, two, three, four, five. . . . It was five, after all. What a jerk, she told herself. She didn't usually do things like that. It was clear that something about Luke was really making her nervous. She hadn't felt like this since—well, not since the early days with Douglas, when she was still downstate at the university.

She turned and cheerfully faced him. "Sugar and cream?"

"That would be fine," he said softly, his eyes never leaving her face.

Darcy scurried toward the refrigerator. "Okay," she said brightly. "One sugar and cream, coming up."

When the coffee had finished dripping into the carafe, Darcy poured two steaming cups and placed them on a teak tray along with the sugar and cream, and together they walked out to the front porch where they could sit and watch the moonlight dance across the field.

"We've talked a lot about me tonight," Darcy said as she slowly stirred her coffee, "but you haven't told me much about yourself. I still don't completely understand why you decided to do a second residency in geriatrics."

"You mean, was there some experience, someone in my life, similar to your grandmother, who sparked my interest in this field?"

Darcy nodded.

"No, nothing like that. I never really knew any of my grandparents. And my parents are still pretty youthful. They live in Arizona, where they enjoy a very active life-style. So it wasn't anything like that, as it was with you—some important older family member. Nothing like that."

"So what—"

"What drew me to geriatrics? I suppose it was a combination of things, but mainly it was realizing—even when I was still in internal medicine—the special problems of the elderly. Some older people, especially the frail elderly, suffer a great deal. In addition to physical pain, often they have lost family members, and then there have been other losses as well. While I was still in my first residency, I began to gravitate toward these patients. I felt that I could help them, and that brought me to geriatrics."

"I can understand that," Darcy said softly. "During the time that I was in nursing school, even before my grandmother got sick, I found myself working more and more with the older patients. Like you, I guess, I just enjoyed the work."

"But then you decided that you wanted to work with them on a more personal basis and not strictly as a nurse. Why was that?"

Darcy was thoughtful for a moment. "It seemed to me that part of growing old, or at least part of the pain of it, was connected with becoming idle. When I was still in nursing school, I would see so many patients who were just doing nothing. They seemed to have given up, lost interest. And yet, they still had so many talents. Their minds were often young and alert. So I thought, 'This is what I want to do. I want to learn why so much inertia seems to set in and what, if anything, I can do to help older people live lives that are more mentally active.' "

She was quiet for a moment as she gazed out across the fields. "After all," she said finally, "older people have such wisdom from all those years of living. It seemed to me that we could all benefit from more programs for them. And I don't just mean programs that provide assistance in health care or in getting around. I wanted to be involved in programs that would help older people to stay active and productive. So that's what I've tried to do both at Good Shepherd and at Towering Oaks."

He looked at her and smiled wryly. "You mean with programs such as your writing group?"

Darcy tried to suppress a smile. "Something like that," she said softly.

"Yes. Well, you know how sorry I am about that."

Darcy looked away. It was still uncomfortable to talk about that day. "Now I do—I guess."

He moved to the edge of his seat. "Just in case you don't, let me explain. You see, when I saw

Louise Ryan crying that day, I thought the whole thing was causing too much stress and—"

Darcy turned and looked at him. "You were right, of course—in thinking that it caused stress, that is. Because of course it did. But don't you see? That's one of the things I'm trying to do— bring a little bit of stress into the residents' lives. Oh, I don't mean a whole lot, naturally—no nervous breakdowns, nothing like that. But just some good, healthy stress." She took a sip of coffee. "Because that's what normal life is, you know. Normal life includes normal stress. And part of what happens at so many nursing homes and retirement villages is that the normal stress of everyday life is simply removed. Life becomes like Jell-o. That's not what I want to have happen. I want to see the residents interacting, talking with one another, reminiscing, anything— just to make their lives more active."

Darcy was perched at the edge of the wicker chair, looking intently at him, and she leaned back now, realizing how carried away she had become. But then, she often got that way when she talked about her work.

"You know that I agree with you, don't you?" Luke asked softly.

Darcy nodded.

"Because I think what you're doing at the two homes is great. It's one of the most innovative programs I've seen—the whole thing—the writing group, the book-discussion group—it's just terrific." For several moments they sat quietly. After a while Luke glanced at his watch. "I'd probably better be getting back," he said as he stood up. "I have rounds early tomorrow morning."

He reached out and took her hand, and together they walked down the porch steps and out to the Thunderbird.

"Thank you for a wonderful evening," Darcy said, looking up at him. "The dinner, the drive to the suburbs—it was all just great!"

"I enjoyed it too." He reached out and, putting both hands on her shoulders, gently pulled her toward him. His kiss was light, like leaves fluttering in an early fall breeze, and Darcy felt her lips soften as her eyes slowly closed and her arms reached up and around his neck. His hold on her tightened as he pulled her more closely to him.

"Darcy," he whispered as he lightly stroked her hair, "you are the nicest thing to come into my life for such a long time." Gradually his grip relaxed, and he took a step backward and looked down at her. "I hope we're going to be seeing more of each other—a lot more."

She looked up at him. It had been a long time since any man had made her feel this way. Not since Douglas. . . .

"I hope so too," she said softly.

He opened the car door and slid behind the wheel. "I'll try to give you a call sometime tomorrow."

"Sounds good," Darcy answered, and as he backed the car out, she stood in the driveway watching. Even after he had swung the car around and headed down the dirt road that led to the highway, she stood quietly watching as the Thunderbird's receding red lights disappeared into the moonlit night.

"Zeke Ryan is very upset," Sue said on Monday morning as Darcy heaved her shoulder bag up on the counter next to the nurses' station.

"Who?" Darcy couldn't imagine what Sue was talking about.

"Zeke Ryan. You know. Louise Ryan's son."

"Oh," Darcy said, remembering the tall, distinguished-looking man from Washington, D.C., who had signed in on the visitors' list. "The one who hadn't been around for so long."

"Right."

"So what's his problem?" Darcy slipped off her jacket and hung it on a nearby hook, then poured herself a cup of coffee. "What's he so upset about?"

"He's upset about his mother." Sue laid her pen down and looked up at Darcy. "You're not going to believe this, but he's afraid she's going to get hurt."

"Get hurt? By whom, for heaven's sake?"

Sue sighed and nervously brushed her hair off her forehead. "By Wadsworth Logan."

Darcy looked at her in disbelief. Wadsworth Logan, the good-natured gentleman who had written the dog story, who was confined to a wheelchair, and who probably wouldn't hurt a fly. "But he wouldn't—"

"I know. He wouldn't hurt a fly. That's what I told Zeke."

"So what's the big—" Darcy paused and looked at her. "Wait a minute. How come you're calling him Zeke already? He just showed up here on Friday."

Sue looked away. "I know."

"So how come—" Darcy looked at Sue more closely. She was sure Sue was blushing.

"How come I called him Zeke? Because I happened to have dinner with him Saturday night, and he—"

Darcy jumped up off her chair. "You *what?*"

"I had dinner with him."

"But you didn't tell me that."

Sue looked at her coyly. "Well, as a good friend of mine said just a few days ago, 'You didn't ask.'"

Darcy plopped back down in her chair. "Touché," she said, remembering her own comment to Sue last week regarding Luke's call. She took a deep breath and looked across the desk at her friend. "Okay. So let's start all over again. On Saturday night you had dinner with Zeke Ryan—who is Louise Ryan's son and who is now known to present company simply as Zeke—and he indicated to you that he thought Wadsworth Logan, of all people, was out to hurt his mother." She leaned back in her chair and sighed. "Sue, you've got to be crazy to go out with this guy. That's the most bizarre notion—"

"No, no. I don't mean that he thought that Wadsworth was intentionally trying to harm his mother or anything like that. It's their—" Sue hesitated. "What should I call it?" She was thoughtful for a moment. "It's their romance that bothers him."

"Their romance! I didn't know—"

"Oh, come on, Darcy! You must have noticed. Louise and Wadsworth go everywhere together."

Darcy remembered how she had seen them talking together out on the terrace last week when she had come in the side door. "Well, yes. I know they're good friends. But a romance? That's the first time I've heard about that."

Sue looked directly at her. "It's for real. Wadsworth and Louise have fallen in love. Louise told that to Zeke on Friday, and Zeke told me."

Darcy took a sip of the lukewarm coffee and made a face. That coffee had probably been sitting there since Friday. She set the Styrofoam cup down on a nearby table. "If that's true, I think it's sort of neat. I just didn't realize. But now that you mention it, they are together a lot. So what's wrong with their falling in love?"

"Nothing's wrong with it. It's just that Zeke is very upset. He's afraid his mother's going to get hurt."

"Oh, now I see what you mean. That kind of hurt. Broken-heart hurt."

"Right. And he's very concerned about it."

"So concerned," Darcy said dryly, "that he hasn't come to visit his mother for nearly two years."

"Now, just a minute." There was a touch of defensiveness in Sue's tone. "There's a reason for that. He's been in the Army, stationed overseas for the past two years. In fact, he just got back to the States a few days before he showed up here at Towering Oaks. So, you see, he hasn't been as neglectful as it might seem."

Darcy smiled. "Been in the Army? A regular Army man, Sue? He didn't just happen to remind you of someone, did he? Someone from your past? Someone you were once married to, maybe?"

"As a matter of fact, he did." Sue looked up

and met her friend's gaze. "In fact, that's probably why I went out with him."

"I figured." The good-natured banter was gone now as the conversation turned more serious. "Because you don't usually go out on dates, especially when it's someone you don't know very well."

Sue smiled shyly. "That's right. I don't." She sighed. "No. There's something different about Zeke. I really like him."

Darcy reached over and gave her hand a squeeze. "That's terrific, and I'm happy for you. He was really nice, then."

Sue nodded. "Very nice. But, of course," she added softly, "you never know." She sighed again. "I suppose time will tell."

"Yes. I'm sure it will." Darcy was thoughtful for a moment as she watched her friend's face. How great it would be, she thought, if Zeke Ryan really turned out to be somebody special for Sue. Sue had been alone for so long.

"So tell me more about Louise and Wadsworth," Darcy prodded finally. "I mean, if they've become close friends and maybe even fallen in love, so what's the problem with that? Why is her son so concerned?"

"Well, it seems that Louise had another romance—maybe ten or so years ago. According to Zeke, she was very much in love with that man. And he seemed to be a nice guy. But then, as the subject of marriage came up, the man simply put an end to the relationship. Wouldn't see Louise anymore, wouldn't talk to her or anything. No reason. He just lost interest. Louise was devastated."

Darcy shook her head. "What a rotten thing to do!" She'd had a similar experience herself, with Douglas, and she knew what it felt like.

"I know. That's why Zeke is so concerned about his mother. It was clear to him that she really is in love. He met Wadsworth and likes him a lot, but because of what happened before, he's really worried that his mother will be hurt again." Sue was silent for a moment, and then she chuckled. "Also, he seemed to wonder exactly what kind of retirement home we're running here—where the residents fall in love and have romances and all that."

"Don't tell me he's got those old stereotypes— that older people never fall in love." Darcy shook her head in disgust. "One thing I really get tired of is this notion that older folks can't fall in love. What an arrogant idea—as though we young people invented love or something!"

Sue nodded. "I agree. But I don't think Zeke feels that way. I honestly think that if he were certain that Wadsworth wasn't just playing with his mother's feelings, and really cared about her, it would ease his mind."

Darcy glanced at her watch. "I've got the writing group in about five minutes—reinstated finally, as you know."

Sue smiled. "Yes, I do know. And that reminds me—I haven't even asked you about your date with Luke. How did it go?"

Darcy stood up. "Super. Absolutely super."

"You really like him?"

Darcy nodded. "Yes. I like him a lot." She smiled down at Sue. "But now I've got to go meet the writing group. We'll talk more later, okay?"

Sue waved in agreement as Darcy headed down the hall toward the seminar room.

Chapter Six

Darcy was just stepping out of the shower when the phone rang. She grabbed a robe and hurried into the bedroom.

"Hi, Darcy. Sorry to call you so early in the morning."

She recognized the voice at once. It was Fidella Ross at Good Shepherd. "That's okay, Fidella." She shoved one arm into her robe. "I was already up." The heat from the farmhouse's furnace hadn't reached the second floor yet, and she shivered slightly as she pulled the robe more tightly around her damp body. "What's up?"

"It's your grandmother."

Darcy could feel every nerve in her body tense up. "What about her?"

"Well, it may be nothing, but I don't like it. When the aide looked in on her a while ago, she didn't seem to be responding. The aide called me, and I went down there. Her vital signs are still okay—well, at least as good as can be expected under the circumstances—though her blood pressure's definitely on the low side. But the main thing is she's simply not responding. I've tried everything." Fidella hesitated. "I just can't get her to wake up."

"Did you call—"

"Dr. Randall? Oh, yes. He was on early rounds over at the hospital. I had the switchboard beep him."

"And what did he say?"

"He said the aide should go back in, maybe wipe her face and neck with a warm cloth, take her vitals again, and then call him back. The aide's down there with her now, and I'm going back in just a minute. But I thought I'd better give you a quick call. I knew you'd want to know."

Even as she talked, Darcy was frantically reaching into her closet for whatever was handy. "You're right, Fidella." She pulled out a brown pantsuit and threw it across the bed. "I'm on my way. And look, if she isn't responding within the next few minutes, call Dr. Randall back right away, okay?"

Fidella said that she would, and Darcy hung up and began hurriedly throwing on whatever clothes she could get her hands on. "Grandma," she whispered frantically as she pulled an old gray sweater over her head, "Grandma, please don't die. Grandma, please, please. . . ."

Within minutes Darcy had backed the red

Bronco out of the drive and was headed down the dirt road that led to the highway. When she hit the expressway, she stepped on the accelerator and, hovering right at the maximum limit, she zipped as fast as she dared along the inside lane. "Please, oh, please, God, don't let anything happen," she whispered over and over as she turned off the expressway and negotiated the familiar turns up the road that led to Good Shepherd.

She pulled into the parking lot a few minutes before seven, and, grabbing her shoulder bag, she jumped out of the car and ran across the lot and up the steps to the nearest entrance.

As she came in the door, she could see Fidella at the other end of the hall. "Fidella," she called as loudly as she dared. After all, she reminded herself, many of the patients might still be sleeping. Fidella turned and waited as Darcy came trotting down the hall. "What's going on now?"

Fidella sighed. "It doesn't look good." Together they headed briskly toward the ARD wing. "Suzanne, the aide, was with her for almost an hour, and since then I've been in and out. We just can't get her to wake up. I think she's gone into a coma, Darcy."

Deep inside, Darcy could feel her heart sink. "You called Dr. Randall back, then."

Fidella nodded. "Yes. He said he'd be here within an hour."

Darcy heaved a sigh of relief as she hurried ahead and into her grandmother's room.

Grandma seemed even smaller than usual, a frail, emaciated little figure lying there on the bed, with a dark-gray hospital blanket tucked securely around her tiny body. Her breathing was steady—a bit louder than usual, Darcy thought—but steady and even.

Gently Darcy took the small, bony hand into her own. "Grandma?" she said softly. "Grandma? Can you hear me, Grandma? It's Darcy."

But there was no answer, no response—just the same steady, somewhat labored breathing.

Darcy turned to Fidella. "I know you've got other things to do. Why don't you go ahead? I'll just sit here with her." She dragged a chair over from a corner of the room and placed it close to the bed. "I'll call if I need you." Fidella nodded in quiet assent as Darcy perched down on the edge of the chair and took one of the tiny hands in hers. "Grandma?" she said softly. "Can you hear me?" But again, there was no response, just the steady, even breathing.

Darcy was still sitting in the same position when Luke arrived. "I'm so glad you're here," she said softly as she looked up at him. "I'm so worried about her."

He reached out and lightly touched Darcy's

shoulder. "I wanted to get here sooner," he said, throwing his coat on a nearby chair, "but a couple of things came up at the hospital. And then I ran into rush-hour traffic."

Darcy nodded. "That's okay. I'm just grateful that you were able to get here this soon."

He leaned over Grandma and studied her face. Gently he pulled each eyelid up and looked at the unseeing eye beneath. Still watching closely, he placed his fingers on the bone just above each eye and exerted a gentle pressure. There was no response. Then he put his stethoscope to his ears and, pulling the blankets down, he listened to her heart. For several moments he stood there, carefully moving the stethoscope to various parts of her chest.

He straightened up and looked across the bed at Darcy. "Her heartbeat is faint and irregular," he said softly. "It's not good." He looked thoughtfully down at the tiny figure and then turned toward the hall, motioning for Darcy to accompany him. "Fidella was right," he said as they stood outside the door. "Your grandmother has gone into a coma."

Darcy lowered her head and gently rubbed her forehead with her fingers. "Does that mean—" she started without looking up.

"That the end is near? It may, and it may not. Unfortunately, it's too early to tell." He reached out and touched her arm. "But I have to tell you—frankly, I'm not optimistic."

Darcy looked up at him quickly, fighting to hold back tears. "But isn't there something we can do?" she asked frantically. "I mean, couldn't we get an ambulance and take her into St. Elizabeth's? Maybe they could do something there."

Luke sighed. "Yes, Darcy, we probably could. We could rush her to the hospital, put her in intensive care, have all kinds of tubes and needles stuck into various parts of her body, and—who knows?—maybe we could keep her alive for weeks, possibly even months." He paused. "But think about it. Is that what you really want? Or, more important, is that what *she'd* really want?"

Darcy shook her head. "I don't know." She felt totally overwhelmed. "I don't know what to say," she said softly.

Fidella came up the hall briskly and joined them.

Luke turned toward her. "You were certainly on target, Fidella. She definitely has gone into a coma. The question now is—is it reversible? And it's too soon to tell—though I have to say that I'm not optimistic."

Darcy looked across at Fidella. "We were just talking about taking her into St. Elizabeth's."

Fidella moved closer to Darcy and put a motherly arm around her shoulders. "Oh, Darcy—

think about it. Your grandmother is, what? Eighty-seven years old?"

"Eighty-eight."

"Eighty-eight. She's had a good life, honey. She was a strong, independent woman. Even though I didn't actually know her then myself, I feel as though I do because you've told me so much about her. Do you think—do you really think—that that strong, beautiful woman would want to spend her final hours—or days— strapped to a bed with a lot of IV needles sticking in her and heaven knows how many tubes?"

Darcy was silent a moment and then she leaned her face against Fidella's shoulder. Without a word Fidella gently wrapped both arms around her. Something about the warm, unspoken understanding of Fidella's gesture caused an unlikely memory to flash out of nowhere and settle in Darcy's mind.

For no reason that she could think of, she saw the field that stretched out so endlessly in front of the old farmhouse, and at that same instant she saw herself, once more a little girl, running across the field, her hand pressed hard against a small arm as she hurriedly trampled through the long grass that grew tall, dotted with daisies and buttercups. Frantically she called for her grandmother, over and over again. A bee—a yellowjacket, really—had stung her on one arm, and the pain was needle-sharp and scary. And then she had reached the edge of the field, and there was Grandma, standing in front of the house, arms outstretched, ready to sweep Darcy up, to hold her close and comfort her.

"It's all right, darling, it's all right," Grandma had said over and over again as she had carried the screaming child into the kitchen. There she had applied packs of ice and baking-soda compresses to the angry, red swelling. Later she had gently extracted the stinger, and Darcy remembered how the pain had subsided as her strong, loving grandmother, who always knew exactly what to do, had gently rocked the sobbing child in her arms until the piercing pain was gone. And now, suddenly, it was as though she were back there again as she quietly sobbed against the understanding shoulder of this kind, gentle nurse.

Finally she stepped back and fumbled for some tissues. Fidella reached into her pocket and pulled out a little purse-pack. "Thanks, Fidella," Darcy said softly as she dabbed at her eyes. Finally she looked up at Luke. "The answer is no, of course," she said softly. "That would be a terrible thing—to put Grandma in intensive care, that is." She wiped her eyes some more. "I was just being selfish, that's all." She looked away as her eyes began to fill up again. "I just can't bear the thought of losing her."

Luke watched her thoughtfully. "But in a way," he asked softly, "haven't you already lost her—a long time ago?"

Darcy looked up at him. "You mean because of the Alzheimer's?"

He nodded.

She sighed. "Yes. Of course I have." She was silent for a moment. "Because by the time I brought her here to Good Shep, she had already gotten to the point where she couldn't take care of herself anymore—even the most personal things. . . ." She stopped and looked away, remembering how terrible it had been to see Grandma, of all people, unable to manage even the simplest task. She sighed. "You're right, of course." She looked up at Luke. "I really lost her a long time ago."

"You did everything you could, Darcy," Fidella said softly. "Nobody could have done more for her than you did."

Darcy reached out and gently squeezed Fidella's hand in silent appreciation. Even though she had known that she had done everything, it was always good to hear those words, to get that reassurance from another person.

Luke turned and started back into Grandma's room. Darcy followed close behind. "I just want to take another look at her," he said as he leaned over the bed. He listened to her heart once more, examined the unseeing eyes, and watched the steady rise and fall of her chest. Her breathing was louder now, more labored, and as Darcy watched, it seemed that her grandmother's color was paler than before.

"I'm going to have Fidella give her a mild pain killer." He looked across at Darcy. "We want to keep her comfortable."

Darcy nodded.

"I don't know how long it will be. Of course, this could be a reversible coma, and she could come to. I doubt that somehow, but it could happen. What are your plans, Darcy? Are you planning to stay here with her?"

"For a while, at least," Darcy said softly. "I was supposed to meet with the book-discussion group this morning, but— Well, I'm sure they'll understand."

"I'm sure they will too," Luke said reassuringly. He glanced at his watch. "I have a couple of other patients to see here, and then I'm going on over to Towering Oaks. I'll explain to Sue Gates what happened and why you may not be in this afternoon." He reached out and gently touched her arm. "And I'll stop by here afterward, before I go back to the hospital."

Darcy looked up at him gratefully. "I'm really glad you're here," she said softly.

"So am I." He gave her an understanding hug and then quietly left the room.

For a long time Darcy sat, still holding her grandmother's tiny hand in hers, patiently watching, silently praying for some movement, some sort of response. But there was nothing— only the loud, steady breathing.

Later in the morning Fidella came into the room and sat with her for a while, and then, with an affectionate squeeze of Darcy's hand, she returned to her other duties. Outside in the hall, Darcy could hear the quiet bustle of the nursing-home routine.

Around eleven, Roy Bogan wheeled tentatively in the door and softly spoke Darcy's name. "Didn't want to bother you, but—"

Darcy looked around. "That's all right, Mr. Bogan. I'm glad to see you."

"I just want you to know that several of us heard about Priscilla and how she sank so low overnight. And we're all thinking about you, Darcy, and praying for you and Priscilla." He wheeled in a little closer and looked for a moment at Grandma's gray, pasty face. He shook his head and then turned and headed back toward the door. Halfway across the room, he stopped and manipulated the chair around again so that he could look at Darcy.

"You know, Darcy, at age one hundred, I face

the possibility of this every night when I go to bed. And each morning when I wake up, I thank the Lord for giving me another day." He hesitated. "Because you know, Darcy, the way I look at it—every day is a gift."

Darcy smiled warmly. Roy Bogan had always been one of her favorite residents, and she was grateful for his gentle understanding and perceptive wisdom. "That's a wonderful attitude, Mr. Bogan. Perhaps that's what helps you to lead such a rich, full life."

"I think maybe it does. But what I'm trying to say is, if it's time for Priscilla to go, just accept it, Darcy, and let her go." He sighed. "I know that's easier said than done, but, still, if the Good Lord says it's her time. . . ." He wheeled his chair closer to Darcy and reached out a thin arm to touch her hand. "Well, who are we to think we know better?"

Darcy smiled appreciatively. "Thank you," she said softly. "I appreciate your telling me that. You're right, of course, and I'm trying hard now to accept it. And, by the way, thank the other residents for their thoughts and prayers too."

"I will, I will," Mr. Bogan said as he turned and wheeled out the door.

Shortly after noon Luke came briskly into the room. "I talked to Sue Gates. She said not to worry about missing today. And she said to give you her love." He walked around to the other side of the bed and looked down at Grandma. "How's she doing now?"

"No better, no worse. Everything's the same as when you were here."

He bent down over Grandma and studied her face. "Priscilla," he said softly. "Can you hear me, Priscilla?" He watched her for a moment and then repeated the words, this time a bit more loudly. He did this several times, and then, with a sigh of frustration, he shook his head and straightened up. "I don't know, Darcy. I don't see a lot of—"

But Darcy hardly heard him. Her eyes still fixed on her grandmother's face, she thought she detected some movement. Without speaking, she lifted her hand to signal to Luke. But he had already caught it, and within a second he had put on his stethoscope and was leaning down again, his eyes fixed on Grandma's face. And then, as though it were the most natural thing in the world, the paper-thin eyelids lifted, and the faded blue eyes looked up and directly at him.

Darcy could hardly believe what she saw. She stood and quickly leaned over the bed. "Grandma," she called. "Grandma, it's Darcy. Can you hear me?"

Slowly her grandmother turned her pale eyes

in Darcy's direction and fixed her gaze on Darcy's face. "Grandma, I'm so glad you're awake," Darcy said, trying to contain her excitement.

As though from far away, Darcy could hear her grandmother try to speak. She bent still closer to the tired face, not wanting to miss a word. She could hear a faint vocal sound, but she couldn't make out the words. She leaned closer. And then, very faintly, she heard her grandmother speak. "Darcy," she said softly.

Darcy couldn't believe it. For more than three years her grandmother had not spoken her name, had never once acknowledged her presence. And now, here she was, looking directly at her and addressing her by name. Darcy's eyes filled as she leaned still closer to the tiny figure. "Yes, Grandma," she said softly. "It's Darcy."

"I'm glad you're here, Darcy," the faint, tiny voice continued. And then, almost as if too tired to go on, the faded eyes began to close. "You were always such a sweet child," she said softly, and then her eyes closed, and with a final sigh, the steady, even breathing resumed.

"Grandma?" Darcy called frantically. "Can you hear me, Grandma?"

But there was no answer, and Darcy looked helplessly across at Luke.

With swift strides he was at her side with one

arm around her shoulders. "Come on, Darcy," he said softly. "Let's go out to the hall."

But when she stood, the tears came as though there were no stopping them, and without a word Luke wrapped his arms around her and gently pulled her to him. Gratefully she pressed her face against the lapel of his sports coat and quietly began to sob.

They stood like that for several moments, his strong arms holding her as her body shook with quiet sobs. Finally he led her out to the hall, where she stood dabbing at her eyes with a tissue. "Wait here a minute, Darcy. I want to look at your grandmother again."

Darcy nodded as she leaned against the wall, still wiping her eyes. Fidella came up the hall and looked at her inquiringly. Briefly Darcy told her what had happened, how her grandmother had recognized her and what she had said.

"That's wonderful," Fidella said softly as she gently squeezed Darcy's hand. "And I don't have to tell you how unusual that is."

Darcy nodded. "I know."

Luke came out of the room and looked at Darcy. But even before he pulled the door shut behind him, she knew what he was going to say.

"She's gone, isn't she?" she said softly. It was more a statement than a question, and the look on his face had already told her what the answer would be.

He nodded as he reached out and gently took her hands in his.

Darcy sighed and looked away. For some reason that she didn't quite understand, the tears were suddenly gone. There were no more sobs building up inside her. In its place was a quiet sense of resignation. Because even though Grandma was gone, Darcy was sure that just before she had died, Grandma had known that she, Darcy, was there with her—just as, when she was little, Grandma had been there for her. And, in those final moments of life, Darcy was sure that Grandma had understood how very much she loved her.

Chapter Seven

During the weeks that followed, Darcy kept to herself somewhat more than usual. Luke called a couple of times to ask her out, once for dinner and another time to a movie. But she found herself a bit more tired than usual and, each time he called, she declined. When they met at work, they usually managed to find a few minutes for coffee together. But Darcy noted, with a kind of detached curiosity, that it had become difficult for her to really enjoy being with him—or with anyone else, for that matter. She wasn't sure just why this was, although she knew that it had something to do with her grandmother's death.

Even with Sue, whom she had known for so many years, Darcy noticed that she was feeling oddly distant and removed. Although she and Sue continued to have an occasional lunch or dinner together, it was becoming more a matter of going through the motions than of really enjoying herself.

And then, on a crisp Saturday afternoon in

mid-October, Darcy stood in the old farmhouse, looking out the front window and across the prairie. A brisk wind swept in from the fields, blowing autumn leaves in every direction and depositing a colorful blanket on her already-covered front yard.

For several moments she stood quietly watching the red and orange leaves accumulate in front of the house. She thought about how, when she was younger, she and her grandmother often spent entire autumn afternoons raking freshly fallen leaves into huge piles. She remembered, too, how they would begin burning the leaves late in the afternoon. As she stood looking out the window, the memory of that delicious aroma of burning leaves swept over her so vividly that it was almost as though she were smelling it now.

Until now, vivid recollections of her grandmother had only made her feel more sad and morose. But this time, for some reason that she didn't quite understand, the muscles in her face seemed to relax as she remembered those golden afternoons, and a quiet sense of peace slowly washed over her. Even some of the tension that she had noticed in her arms and legs began to loosen. It was almost as if a fresh October breeze had just rippled through the old farmhouse, Darcy thought curiously, sweeping out sadness and replacing it with a quiet feeling of tranquility and well-being.

Perhaps it was finally time to do some raking, she decided, and she turned and started for the hall closet. A light jacket would be just fine for a day like this. Out in the kitchen, the phone rang loudly. She caught it on the second ring.

"Are you busy?" a familiar male voice asked tentatively.

"Luke!" Darcy was surprised at how good his voice sounded to her.

"I'm over here at Towering Oaks—about ready to head home. But I decided to give you a try before I left. If you're not busy, I thought I might drop over and say hello." He hesitated. "Maybe even lure you out for pizza later—if you're not tied up."

"Sounds great," she said happily. "I'd love to see you."

"Terrific. I'll be by in about half an hour."

Humming to herself, Darcy headed out the front door, closing it firmly behind her against the brisk wind. As she rounded the corner toward the garage, she noticed one of her rakes leaning against the side of the house. Funny, she thought. She didn't remember leaving that rake out, though she probably had put it there yesterday while doing some tidying in the garage. In any case, finding it now saved her a trip to the

garage, and she picked up the rake and contentedly set to work, coaxing stray clumps of leaves
toward a pile in the middle of the yard.

A while later she looked up and across the
field. The afternoon sun was already low in the
southern sky, and the breeze that intermittently
swept in across the prairie seemed brisker than
before. Not the best day for raking, she told herself as she watched the leaves swirl around. It
seemed as though she no sooner got them into
some sort of a neat pile then a gust of wind blew
them all over the place again. At the same time,
she knew that it didn't really matter. She was enjoying the task, and for some reason that she
couldn't quite put her finger on, she felt totally
contented and at peace.

Down at the end of the dirt road, a car turned
off the highway and headed up toward the farmhouse. She glanced at her watch. Probably Luke,
she thought happily. She rested the rake against
the side of the house and waved cheerfully as the
gray Thunderbird came into view.

He pulled into the driveway and quickly
opened the door. Darcy felt an overwhelming
sense of joy as she briskly walked around the
front of the car to meet him. A wide, boyish grin
spread across his face as their eyes met, and he
spread out his arms in warm invitation. Without
a second's hesitation she rushed into them, her

own arms sliding easily around him. For a moment he held her close, and then finally he gently kissed her forehead and stepped back.

"Well," he said, smiling down at her, "if I didn't say it before, hello! It's good to see you." He leaned down and lightly kissed her again. "You're looking gorgeous—as usual."

Darcy pushed a stray lock off her forehead and smiled up at him. "Now I know why I like having you around—you always say such nice things!"

Casually he draped his arm around her shoulders as they walked up the steps of the front porch and sat down on the old glider. He looked out across the front yard. "Looks like you've been doing some raking."

"Well, I started to." Darcy laughed as a sudden gust of autumn wind blew in across the prairie, scattering her neatly raked pile of leaves.

He moved forward on the glider. "Got some large plastic bags? We could try to bag them before they all blow away."

She shook her head. "Let them go. I wasn't working all that long, anyway. And look—" She pointed to the swirling leaves. "There's another gust. They'll all be gone in a moment. Anyway, it was fun raking them, and that's what counts." A sudden chill whipped across the front porch, and Darcy gave a tiny shiver. "Let's go in and have coffee. It's getting chilly out here."

Inside, they sat at Darcy's kitchen table, enjoying huge mugs of rich, hot coffee. Luke leaned forward and helped himself to one of the homemade cookies from the platter that Darcy placed in the center of the table. He took a bite and then held the cookie in front of him and looked at it appreciatively. "Good," he said softly. "What kind are they?"

"Oatmeal and raisin. I made them this morning."

He took another bite. "They're absolutely delicious." He finished it off and reached for another. "I know I shouldn't. . . ." He patted his firm midriff. "But what the heck—maybe I can run an extra mile tomorrow to make up for it."

Darcy laughed delightedly. "Luke! Give me a break!" She shook her head. "Imagine you—with a weight problem!" She glanced admiringly at his strong, muscular body. "I can't imagine you ever being overweight!"

He smiled and stirred his coffee. "Well, if you're right—and I'm not saying that you are, mind you—it's because I work out every day. There's a three-mile jogging path in the woods near where I live. I run it three or four mornings a week."

Darcy watched him admiringly. "That's terrific." She took a sip of coffee. "And I run down the old dirt road behind the house almost every day before I go into work. It's about a mile each way."

He leaned back in his chair as he finished his cookie. "So that's why you always look so fantastic." He watched her quietly. "Not to mention being a fabulous cook, a gorgeous woman, a great conversationalist, and, of course—last but not least—a warm, lovable, very caring human being." He leaned forward and took one of her hands in both of his. "You know how I feel about you, don't you?"

It was more a statement than a question, and Darcy gave a nod as their eyes met and locked. "You mean a great deal to me, Darcy. If I haven't said it before, it's not because I haven't felt it." He squeezed her hand. "Or wanted to."

"I know," she said quietly. "And I feel the same way." She reached out her free hand and put it on top of his. He tightened his grip in response. "You mean a lot to me too, Luke. And have, for a long time." Probably since that warm, wonderful morning just before the end of summer, she thought, when she had come striding briskly down the hall at Good Shep and had first seen him, standing there at the nurses' station.

"I've wanted to tell you before—that I thought I was falling in love with you, that is," he said.

Darcy nodded and looked away. She understood why he hadn't, and she felt a burst of love and affection for his patience and understanding. "But you didn't," she said softly, "because of—"

"Because of your grandmother," he finished for her.

She looked across at him in silent gratitude. "You were right to wait," she said quietly.

He nodded. "I know that. And I knew it then. Sometimes—honestly—I have wanted so much to take you in my arms and hold you and comfort you and kiss your tears away."

They were quiet for a moment as they looked at each other in silent understanding. "But you knew, didn't you, that I just wasn't ready yet?"

"You needed time. I understood that. But you'll never know how helpless I felt sometimes, watching you feeling so down. I wanted so much to do something."

She smiled gently across at him. "But of course there was nothing that you—or anyone, for that matter—could do." She sighed. "I just had to work it out myself."

"That's right. You were grieving." He hesitated. "I knew that you needed some space and quiet to do it in." He sighed. "It was tough sometimes. Because I wanted so much to rush in and help you through it. But of course I couldn't. Deep down I always knew that. Grief is just something that we all have to work out for ourselves, in our own time and our own way."

"But today. . . ." She looked at him inquiringly. "Today—it was as though you seemed to know. . . ."

He smiled gently. "I did. When I came up the road this afternoon and saw you there, raking those leaves. . . ." He chuckled. "Even with that crazy wind blowing every which way—you just looked happy. Contented. Like you had somehow come to grips with it."

She took a deep breath and then looked directly at him. "You were right, of course. I think perhaps I have." She hesitated. "I guess it's as though I'm finally beginning to understand— that Grandma really is gone, that it's over, and that it's time for me to begin picking up the pieces of my life and get on with it." She was quiet for a moment. "I know that's what Grandma would have wanted."

"I'm sure it is."

"You know, Luke, it's funny. But it was almost as though I heard her—Grandma, that is." She shook her head in mild embarrassment. "I know this must sound crazy, but— Well, you're right. Things *were* different today—especially today. Because this afternoon, after I did some laundry and baked the cookies, I was standing right over there, by the living-room window." She motioned toward the front room. "And I saw all the leaves that had blown into the yard, and then it was almost as though I heard her—heard Grandma, that is. It was as though she were telling me, 'Darcy, look at all those leaves out there. Remember how you and I used to go out and rake them together? And how much fun we used to have?' " Darcy stopped and looked across at Luke. "Does this sound crazy?"

He shook his head. "No. It doesn't sound crazy at all."

"And then I remembered how, when I was a little girl, sometimes we'd rake the leaves into a big pile, and then I'd put down my rake and run across the yard and jump right into them. And Grandma would laugh and laugh. Because, you see, she never really cared so much about the leaves—about whether they were raked—as she did about whether we were enjoying what we were doing. Everything she did—whether it was raking leaves or growing vegetables or making a casserole—she always enjoyed it. That was what life was all about, she used to tell me, making every day as good as you could make it. Harvesting the days, she used to call it."

"That's a nice expression—harvesting the days. I like that." He was thoughtful for a moment. "Anyway, so you thought about all this today, and then you decided to go out and rake leaves. No wonder you looked so happy when I first saw you out there."

Darcy nodded. "I *was* happy. Because I didn't care if the wind blew the leaves around or not. Just like Grandma never cared if I jumped into the leaf pile and messed them all up. Because it was raking them and enjoying it—that's what mattered. So that was how I was feeling when you saw me today." She sighed contentedly. "I was just enjoying raking them."

Luke squeezed her hand. "And it showed. You were positively radiant."

She smiled across at him. "And there was something else too." She looked away. "I hope this doesn't sound too silly."

"Try me," he said gently.

"Well, after you called and I went outside—as I was going around the side of the house and over toward the garage to get a rake—there. . . ." Darcy looked away in embarrassment. "Honestly, you're going to think I'm crazy."

"No, I won't."

"Well, there, leaning up against the side of the house— Now, please understand, Luke. I'm sure I must have put it there myself. It's just that— well, I just don't happen to remember doing it, at least not right now, anyway. But I'm sure that's how it got there."

"How what got there?"

"The rake. Grandma's rake. It was leaning up against the side of the house. I must have put it there myself, probably yesterday afternoon, after work, because I tidied up the garage a bit, and I probably just took it out and leaned it against the house and forgot to put it back."

Luke nodded. "Probably."

"But even so, it was wonderful. It was almost like an invitation or something. As if Grandma were saying, 'Come on, Darcy—enough of this grieving business. You get out here and enjoy yourself. The way you used to when you and I would rake leaves together.' " She looked across at Luke, no longer even trying to hide the tears of joy in her eyes. "It was as if she were telling me that it was time for me to start living again—and not to be afraid."

Luke squeezed her hands. "Afraid?" he asked softly. "Afraid of what?"

She was quiet for a moment. "Afraid of loss. Afraid of caring for people and then losing them. First my parents, you know, and now Grandma. . . ." She withdrew her hand and reached into her pocket for a tissue. "For a while there it was beginning to seem to me that every time I really cared about someone. . . ."

"You lost that person?"

She dabbed at her eyes and nodded.

"But now you don't feel that way anymore?"

"No—at least not the way I did. Because I just know what Grandma would say if I could talk to her. In fact, as I stood there looking out the window earlier this afternoon, it was almost as if I heard her." She looked across at him. "Though, of course, I know that it was really coming from inside me," she added quietly.

He nodded. "Of course."

"Anyway, it was almost as if I heard her telling me that, of course, there might be loss again— that's a risk that I'm going to have to take. After all, there are no guarantees in life. Life is filled with risks, and if I am going to live, risk is part of the rules of the game." She looked across at him. "It was just as if she were saying all that to me. I hope this doesn't sound too foolish," she added quietly.

"Of course not. What it sounds like is that you've just moved into the final stage of your grief, that's all. It sounds like you've moved into acceptance. You have accepted the fact that your grandmother is gone, that she's not coming back, and you have accepted the fact that now it's time for you, Darcy, to get on with your life—risks and all."

"That's just the way it feels." She was quiet for a moment. "But you know, Luke—the rake. I just don't understand that. Because, honestly, I don't remember. . . ."

"It doesn't matter, Darcy. What you've described is very common. Don't you remember that from your work in gerontology? That sometimes as we reach the final stage of our grieving process, something happens and it seems like—"

"A sign," Darcy interrupted him.

He nodded.

"Of course. I'd forgotten that." She was thoughtful for a moment as she remembered back to all she had studied about grief. "I remember now. Sometimes, as people are coming out of the final stage of their grieving process, something happens—like the rake this morning. And, to the person, it almost seems that he or she has been given a sign. But of course—"

"Of course, it's a coincidence of some sort. We all know that." He gave her hand a squeeze. "But it's funny, isn't it—how often it happens. . . ."

Darcy watched him thoughtfully. "Yes," she said softly. "And how very wonderful and freeing it is."

Much later, they sat on the living-room sofa, watching the flickering embers in the large stone fireplace. "You know, this has been a wonderful afternoon and evening." Luke turned toward Darcy and slipped his arm around her shoulders. "It was a great dinner—not to mention good conversation and terrific company."

Darcy smiled up at him. "I've enjoyed it too.

It's given us a chance to get to know each other even better."

He wrapped his other arm around her and pulled her more closely to him. "And, you know, the more I learn, the more I like."

"And I think I can say exactly the same thing," she said happily.

"Good!" He gave her a hug. "I'm glad to hear that."

They sat quietly together for several minutes. Finally Luke bent down and gently took her chin in his hand. Turning her face toward his, he leaned forward and kissed her lightly on the lips. Almost without realizing it, her arms crept up and around his neck. Gradually she could feel his grip on her tighten as he kissed her again and again.

"Sweetheart," he said huskily, and Darcy let her head rest against his shoulder. His arms felt warm and secure, and she felt as though she could stay like this forever. "I'm afraid it's time for me to hit the road." He moved toward the edge of the sofa. "I'm on call tomorrow morning, and, unfortunately, it's getting late."

Reluctantly they stood up and, hand in hand, walked to the front door. "Again," he said as he slipped on his coat, "it's been a wonderful day and evening. And I'm really glad that you're working through your grief. It seems like the worst is behind you, like you really have come to terms with it."

She looked up at him. "I think I have," she said softly. "And, if I haven't said it before, I'm grateful to you for helping me through it."

He leaned down and kissed her again. "I'm glad I was here for you."

After promising to call her the next day, he opened the large oak door and stepped out onto the porch. A biting wind whipped across the field and in through the house.

"Brrr," Darcy said, wrapping her arms around her slender body. "A cold front must have moved in."

He leaned down and kissed her one final time and then started to pull the door shut behind him. "Don't stand here—you'll freeze." Darcy agreed and, after a quick good-bye, she closed the door behind him.

But long after the Thunderbird's rear lights had disappeared down the dirt road, she stood by the window, watching the brisk autumn wind whip the leaves around the yard. Finally she turned and, after lowering the thermostat and snapping off the lights, she slowly made her way up the creaky old stairs to bed.

*　　*　　*

"I need to talk to you about something," Sue Gates said when Darcy arrived at Towering Oaks on Monday afternoon.

Darcy looked at her in surprise. Immediately she thought of the developing relationship between Zeke Ryan and Sue, and she hoped that nothing had gone wrong between them.

"It's nothing serious," Sue hurriedly reassured her. "That is, nothing that probably won't work out in time. But still, I'd like to get some input from you."

"No problem," Darcy said, hanging up her coat. "Are you free later on—say, right after we get out of work?"

Sue indicated that that would be fine, and the two agreed to meet at a nearby coffee shop. "A little after five," Darcy called over her shoulder as she headed down the hall toward the seminar room, and Sue nodded in agreement.

All of the writing group's participants had gathered and were sitting around the large oak table when Darcy walked in.

"Hello, Darcy." "Hi there, Darcy." "How're you doing, dear?" several of the residents called out as she walked to the side of the table and took her usual place between Henry Van Dusen and Louise Ryan.

"Hi, everybody." She smiled happily as she looked around the table. Since her grandmother's death she had not been meeting the group with her usual regularity, and although she knew that they all understood, she also could tell they were as glad to have her back as she was to be there.

"You're looking a lot better, Darcy," Helen-Marie Wiggins said as she leaned forward and smiled.

Darcy smiled back at her. "Thanks, Mrs. Wiggins. I'm feeling a lot better too." She looked around the table. "And I want to thank all of you for the nice notes and cards you sent. It meant a lot."

"Well, you're talking to a group of people who understand what you've been through, Darcy," Henry Van Dusen said quietly. "After all, you can't live to our ages and not go through some loss."

The group murmured in agreement.

Darcy looked around the table at the warm, understanding faces that surrounded her. For a few seconds the group lapsed into silence. Suddenly Darcy found herself looking away and down at her hands, resting quietly in her lap. Something had happened during those few seconds. She wasn't sure just what it was, but she knew that a very strong and powerful feeling had swept over her, and she found herself struggling to hold back tears.

The group understood, she thought. It was just

as Henry Van Dusen had pointed out. When you get to be older, as the members of this group were, there isn't much that you haven't been through, that you don't understand. They knew what it was like to lose someone very dear. They knew because it had happened to them. They had had many losses—many more than she—and they were stronger and wiser because of it.

"Suffering brings growth," Grandma had told her once when the subject of Darcy's parents' early deaths had come up. "That's just the way it works. It's as though something out there is saying, 'I'm going to bend you and twist you and stretch you in a whole lot of different ways, and sometimes it's going to hurt—a lot. But if I don't, you'll just stay the same. You'll never grow.' That's the price we humans pay, Darcy—for growing up, for becoming all that we can be."

Beside her, Louise Ryan reached out and gave Darcy's hand an affectionate squeeze. Darcy looked at her in quiet appreciation. These were her friends, she thought as she looked around the room. How lucky she was to know and work with these gentle, understanding people!

She reached into her pocket for a tissue and gently blew her nose. "Well. . . ." She shifted her position and looked around the room. "Perhaps it's time for us to get started." She cleared her throat self-consciously. "So—who's got something to read?"

There was a moment of silence, and then, finally, Henry Van Dusen's hand went up. "I have."

"Great!" Darcy said. "Let's hear it."

Henry adjusted his glasses and looked around the room. "It's another poem," he said firmly, almost as though he were daring someone to challenge him.

"Wonderful!" one of the participants said in quiet encouragement.

"Your poems are so good, Henry," Louise Ryan added as she turned her attention toward him. "We always look forward to them."

Henry cleared his throat. " 'October Harvest,' " he said loudly as he looked around the table. "That's the title." Several of the participants murmured appreciatively.

"Nice title, Henry," someone said.

"Very appropriate for the season," another agreed.

" 'October Harvest,' " he repeated, and then he was silent for a couple of seconds before he began to read:

I sat looking out of my window
From my tiny room.

The stars were out, the sky was bright,
Reflecting a full harvest moon.

And my thoughts drifted back to my child-
   hood,
When I was a small, young lad.
I remembered my sisters and brothers,
And I thought of my mother and dad.

For on nights like this, when the harvest
   moon
Would fill the heavens with light,
My dad would go out and hitch up the
   team
And plow far into the night.

During harvesttime we'd gather the corn,
And we'd pick up the barley and hay.
We'd bundle each load and tie it up right
And store it all safely away.

Then winter would come, bringing ice
   storms and snow,
And we'd thank the Good Lord up above
For blessings we had, each warm, caring
   face—
Our bountiful harvest of love.

The group broke into spontaneous applause.

"Wonderful, Henry," someone said. "Your best yet," another agreed. "It's just excellent," someone else added.

Henry Van Dusen sat, trying to suppress his delight. "Thank you, folks," he said gruffly. "Thank you very much." But the group was reluctant to stop, and the applause continued.

"You know, Darcy," Louise Ryan said when the room finally quieted down, "I hate to sound boastful, but I really think we have all gotten very good."

Several members of the group laughed good-naturedly.

Louise looked around. "Well, what I mean is—we've improved so much."

"We sure have," Wadsworth Logan said, nodding in agreement.

"There's no doubt about it," Helen-Marie Wiggins agreed enthusiastically. "We're so much better than when we first started out. Thanks to you, Darcy."

Darcy shook her head. "No, I haven't done it. It's you folks—you're the ones with the talent, not me."

"Well, dear, you've given us the encouragement," Louise said.

"And the confidence," Wadsworth added. "And speaking of confidence, that leads me to something I'd like to read."

"Great!" someone said.

"Let's hear it, Wadsworth," another member added encouragingly.

"Well, this isn't a poem, like Henry's. And it isn't a story, like I've read before." A trace of a smile began to creep across Wadsworth's face. "And it isn't even an essay or the first chapter of a novel or—"

"For heaven's sake," Helen-Marie interrupted impatiently, "what in the world is it, then?"

Wadsworth's face broke into a huge smile as he turned toward Louise, who was sitting beside him. "Shall I go ahead and read it, Louise?" he asked softly.

To Darcy's surprise, a trace of red began to creep up Louise's face as she suddenly gazed down at her hands, neatly folded in her lap. Without looking up, she nodded.

Reaching into the side pocket of his jacket, Wadsworth pulled out a folded piece of lined yellow paper. He spread it carefully before him and cleared his throat. "This is for everyone here." He looked around the room. "For all of you— our friends and loved ones."

The room became suddenly still.

"Mr. Wadsworth Logan and Mrs. Louise Ryan," he began in his most solemn voice, "request the honor of your presence at their marriage at Towering Oaks Retirement Village on Thanksgiving Day—"

He got no further. The place dissolved into bedlam.

"Your marriage?" someone said in delighted disbelief.

"Louise! Wadsworth!"

"Here—at Towering Oaks? Thanksgiving? Oh, that's just beautiful!"

Across the table, Henry chuckled happily. "You old devil, Wadsworth! I didn't know. . . . I mean, I knew you two were close, but I didn't know you were *that* close!"

"Oh, this is wonderful," Helen-Marie said, reaching for a tissue. "Just think—we'll actually have a wedding, right here, at Towering Oaks."

Darcy sat stunned by the news. Like the others, she knew that Louise and Wadsworth were good friends—enough, even, to concern Louise's son, Zeke—but she had no idea that a romance of this nature was brewing.

Delighted, she leaned toward Louise and gave her a hug. "That's the most wonderful news I've heard in—I don't know how long!" And she gave her another quick hug. "I'm so happy for you two."

"Thank you, Darcy," Louise said, wiping away a trace of a tear. "I think I can honestly say that I haven't been this happy for many,

many years." She turned back toward Wadsworth and slipped her hand into his.

The group spent the rest of the time discussing the news, and, finally, Darcy suggested that there was too much excitement for them to get any more serious work done. The group agreed, and they broke up early, each one—with the help of their canes and walkers—heading cheerfully back down the hall toward the dayroom.

After she had seen that the last person had gotten safely down to the dayroom, Darcy returned to the seminar room and started putting the chairs back in order. Love, she thought happily as she looked around at the disarray of chairs and the tiny wads of tissue here and there. It didn't matter whether you were in your twenties, as she and Luke were, or in your fifties, as Sue and Zeke were, or in your eighties, as Louise and Wadsworth were. There were no two ways about it. Love, she thought as she slipped the last chair under the table and looked contentedly around the room, was the glue that held us all together. Love was wonderful.

Chapter Eight

"So—I guess you heard about Wadsworth Logan and Louise Ryan," Darcy said. She and Sue were sitting in a corner booth at the nearby Cozy Café. "Isn't it exciting!"

Sue stirred her coffee thoughtfully. "Not if you ask Zeke, it isn't."

"Why not? I'd think he'd be—"

"Pleased? Excited?" Sue sighed. "Guess again!"

Darcy looked at Sue in surprise. "I don't get it."

"Well, let me begin at the beginning. You see, Zeke and I have been seeing quite a lot of each other these past few weeks. I would have told you more about it, but with your grandmother's passing and all. . . ."

"I know. I guess I've been keeping to myself a lot during this last month. But now—at least since last weekend—I think I've finally come to grips with it."

"It shows," Sue said, smiling. "I could tell as

soon as I saw you this morning. You looked a lot better—more like your old self."

"Well, that's how I'm beginning to feel. Finally. Anyway, tell me more about you and Zeke. Is it serious?"

"Yes. At least it's more serious than anything else that's happened to me in the last twenty years."

Darcy smiled in delight. "That's great, Sue."

"I thought so too. Until a couple of days ago, anyway."

"Why? What happened then?"

"That was when Zeke's mother told him that she and Wadsworth wanted to get married at Thanksgiving."

"And Zeke didn't like that? Why on earth not?"

"Well, I can't exactly say that he didn't like it. Let's just say that it's given him problems." She sighed. "Frankly, I can't quite figure it out. After all, it isn't as though Zeke doesn't know Wadsworth. In fact, he's met him several times, met his family, even, and he seems to like them all a lot. But—well, I don't know. He just seems so darn uneasy about the whole thing. As though something terrible might come of it."

Darcy was thoughtful for a moment. "You don't suppose Zeke's just having a more or less normal reaction to his mother's proposed marriage."

"How do you mean?"

"Oh, I remember in one of my gerontology courses at St. Monica's—I think it was in a psychology course—we were discussing various family members' adjustment to aging parents. I remember that one of the things that can really have an impact on adult children is when the older parent unexpectedly decides to remarry."

Sue was thoughtful for a moment. "You know, I remember learning about that too. Sometimes the adult children really have a time with that, don't they?"

"Right. At first it often hits them as something that's a bit discordant, almost as though the older parent shouldn't be even considering such a thing. That's partly because they've come to think of the parent as the child and consider themselves the parent. But after a while they usually come to accept it, once they get used to the idea—providing, of course, that they basically like the person the parent is planning to marry, which seems to be true in this case."

"No doubt about it. Zeke really does like Wadsworth. And when you think about it, who wouldn't? Wadsworth is a great guy."

"I'll bet with time he'll work it through. Especially someone like Zeke. Because from everything you've said, he sounds like a really nice guy."

Sue smiled across the table. "He's terrific, Darcy. I like him a lot."

"That's great!" Darcy said, happy for her friend. "I'm sure this problem will work out."

Sue nodded. "I guess you're right. Zeke just has to get used to the fact that even though his mother is no longer living totally on her own, she's still an adult, just as he is, with the same rights to make major decisions that he has. I'll broach the subject with him when I see him tonight—see how that goes over."

"Sounds like a good idea." Darcy paused while a waitress refilled her coffee cup. "So what about you two? No chance of a double wedding at Thanksgiving, is there?"

Sue laughed. "No—nothing that soon, anyway. After all, we've known each other for only a couple of months. But later on—well, you never know. I've got to admit—we have talked about it, a little bit, anyway."

"Sue! That's wonderful. Don't tell me he's proposed already?"

"No, I wouldn't say that. But we have talked about the future—our future. You see, Zeke will be retiring from the Army in January. He had already planned to settle in this area, mainly so that he could be closer to his mother."

"Terrific! So maybe later on. . . ."

Sue smiled. "Maybe. We'll see. And speaking of getting serious, what about you and Luke?"

"He's become really important to me, Sue."

"Well, I've got to tell you—when he was at Towering Oaks this morning, I thought to myself how much more relaxed he looked than when he started out with us. Remember how stern and unbending he seemed then?"

"Do I ever!"

"But today he seemed relaxed, almost mellow. He looked really happy. And, by the way, he just raves about the writing group now. He was saying just a few days ago that he was certainly mistaken when he thought that all the reminiscing that went on in the group caused undue stress. He said that the benefits clearly outweighed any drawbacks."

Darcy smiled. "I figured he'd come around—in time."

They talked some more about recent events, and then, realizing that it was getting late, they paid for their coffee and left, promising to get together for more time during the weekend.

The Littlefield County Animal Shelter van was already in the parking lot at Good Shepherd when Darcy pulled in on Thursday morning. She was glad to see it there. The animal-visitation program had been so successful for both the animals and the patients that Pete Hiller, the shelter's administrator, had agreed to bring some of the animals back for a regular, second weekly visit.

As usual, the dayroom was alive with excitement. Roy Bogan sat in his wheelchair near the door, contentedly petting a small, very thin tan-and-white cat. He looked up as Darcy entered the room. "Look at this little guy, Darcy. Isn't he something?"

Darcy pulled up a chair and sat down. "Well, hello there," she said as she scratched one of the cat's ears. "What's his name, Mr. Bogan?"

"I was asking Pete that, but he says this little guy doesn't even have a name yet. He just came into the shelter a couple of days ago. He's quite old, you know. That's why he's so thin. Pete says he's got to be close to twelve or thirteen. Seems somebody found him wandering along the side of a road and brought him in." He stroked the cat affectionately.

"If he doesn't have a name, why don't you name him?"

Roy looked at her quizzically. "Do you think it would be all right if I did?"

"I'll bet Pete would be delighted."

"You think so?"

"Sure. But if you want, I'll go over and ask

him." She nodded toward the far side of the room where Pete was doing obedience demonstrations with a golden retriever. "You want me to?"

Roy nodded. "That would be very nice, Darcy. I guess if I could name him, it would almost make it seem like this little guy was mine." He went on affectionately stroking the purring cat.

Darcy stood up. "I'll be right back."

As she expected, Pete said it would be fine for Roy to name the cat. "In fact, it would be a real help." Pete waved across the room at Roy as he nodded enthusiastically. "It would save the staff from trying to think up a new name for still another animal."

"You hear that?" Darcy said as she returned to Roy's side. "Pete would be delighted to have you name the cat."

Roy chuckled. "Well, then, I'll have to give the matter some thought. I don't want to name such a handsome cat just any old thing."

Darcy reached down and touched his shoulder. "Take your time, Mr. Bogan. I'll check back with you in a little while."

She moved around the room, pausing to talk to a group of residents who had gathered around a mother dog contentedly nursing five tiny puppies. As she made the rounds, several of the residents reached up from wheelchairs to squeeze her hand sympathetically, expressing an unspoken but still lingering sympathy for her recent loss. Even though it had been more than a month now, Darcy appreciated their warm concern and quiet understanding.

When she returned to Roy's side, the thin little cat had gathered himself into a tiny ball as he slept contentedly on Roy's lap. "So, do you have a name yet?" she asked as she sat down.

Roy nodded. "I'm going to name him Odysseus."

"Why, that's a wonderful name! How did you ever happen to think of that?"

Roy was quiet for a moment. "Well," he said finally, "you know, Odysseus was a man who went on a long, long journey."

Darcy nodded.

"Odysseus traveled everywhere and saw everything. Sort of like me. I've lived a long time, you know, Darcy, a real long time—one hundred years now. Just think of that! Why, I was in the First World War, saw action in France, even lived in foxholes. And still I'm hanging in there." He looked down fondly at the scrawny cat. "It's the same with this little guy here. He's been through a lot too. Because heaven only knows where he was before he got to that road where somebody finally found him—or, even, how he got there. And there's no telling how many adventures he's had in his life—or troubles, either.

This little guy—he reminds me of myself." He looked up at her, his faded eyes watering.

Darcy reached out and gently put her hand on his.

"So the two of us, him and me, well, we're survivors. Same as Odysseus in the story—he was a survivor too. And, like Odysseus, this little guy and I, well, we've been everywhere, seen everything, and still we just go on. We don't give up." He reached into his pocket for a handkerchief. "I always liked the story of Odysseus. He was a strong man—lived a full life."

"He was like you, Mr. Bogan."

Roy blew his nose noisily. "I'd like to think so, Darcy. I've sure done my best—to go full circle, that is."

Darcy tightened her grip on his hand. "You've done that, Mr. Bogan. And you're still doing it. I don't know how you do it, but you never seem to let things get you down."

The cat squirmed slightly and then contentedly resettled himself on Roy's lap. "That's because I'm tough—just like this little guy here is tough. And I know that each day has got to be lived as it comes. Get as much out of each day as you can—that's the real secret of life." He paused and looked up at Darcy. "Because each day is a gift, you know."

"That's exactly what my grandmother used to

say," Darcy said softly. "Harvest the days, she used to tell me."

"Well, she was right." He was thoughtful for a moment. "Priscilla was tough too. She understood the secret." He looked down at the cat as he stroked it affectionately. "And this little guy, in his own way, he understands it too."

Darcy was quiet for a moment. Finally she reached out with her free hand and gently scratched the sleeping cat. "Odysseus. That's a fine name, Mr. Bogan."

"Glad you like it. And by the way, do you think maybe Pete would bring Odysseus with him whenever he comes out? I know he usually brings different animals with him each time, but maybe he'd make an exception with Odysseus."

"I'm sure he will." She gave his hand a gentle squeeze as she stood up. "But let me go and ask him to be sure."

At the other end of the room, she explained Roy's request to Pete. "No problem," Pete said, delighted that the cat now had both a name and a friend. "That cat is too old for adoption, you know. But when any of the patients in one of the nursing homes that we visit takes a special liking to an animal, well, that sort of gives that animal a reprieve—if you know what I mean."

Darcy nodded.

"It gives us an excuse to keep the animal and

to go on caring for him—even when the animal is much too old for adoption. Anyway, Dr. Williams, the shelter's vet, is due in this afternoon. I'll tell him to give Odysseus a real careful going-over. Maybe with some good veterinary care and all this love and affection from Roy, we can build up the little fellow. So tell Roy he can count on it—Odysseus will be with us each time from now on."

"That's the best thing that could happen," Fidella said later in the morning when Darcy told her about Roy's attachment to the cat. "You know, I love the days when Pete comes to Good Shepherd. I can't believe the good those animals do the patients. Everybody seems relaxed and mellow for the rest of the day."

Darcy nodded. "It's really something, isn't it? I guess it makes the residents feel needed."

"And loved, Darcy. These animals give so much love. All you have to do is pet one of them, and it's like you're their friend for life. Next to the discussion groups, the animal-shelter visit is just about the best program you've set up here. Because everybody wins—the patients, the animals, and even the staff. It's great!"

Darcy parked the Bronco in the underground garage at Towering Oaks and, shunning the elevator, took the steps up to the main floor two at a time. She was eager to see Sue, hoping to hear that Zeke was feeling more comfortable about his mother's planned Thanksgiving wedding.

But as soon as she opened the door and stepped out to the main floor, she knew something was wrong. At the far end of the hall, she could see Zeke standing with his arms around his mother, who was quietly sobbing against his shoulder. Several of the aides were scurrying in various directions, and along the side of the hall she could see some of the patients, leaning on walkers or canes, anxiously watching all the activity.

She turned up the nearest corridor to head toward the nurses' station and almost ran into Helen-Marie Wiggins, who was standing to one side, tensely gripping her walker.

"Oh, Darcy!" she said anxiously. "Did you hear what happened?"

Darcy shook her head.

"Wadsworth Logan—he had a heart attack."

"Oh, no!"

"About two hours ago. We were all sitting in the lounge, watching one of the talk shows, and all of a sudden Wadsworth let out a little moan and clutched his chest, and then the next thing anyone knew, he was all slumped over in his wheelchair."

"How awful! Was Sue Gates there?"

"No, but one of the aides was. She ran and got

Sue. Sue and the aides really worked fast. They began giving him this—what do you call it?—CPR?"

Darcy nodded. "Cardio pulmonary resuscitation. Was Sue able to revive him?"

"No. Poor Wadsworth—he never stirred." She lowered her voice. "In fact, to tell you the truth, Darcy, he looked just awful. One of the aides ran and called the ambulance. I'll tell you—I never saw anything so fast. The paramedics were there in less than ten minutes. Put him on a stretcher and off they went, siren blasting, lights flashing, and everything."

Darcy leaned her head against the wall. "What a terrible thing!"

"Yes, it was," Helen-Marie went on. "And, of course, it was especially bad for poor Louise. She was sitting right next to Wadsworth when it happened. They're always together, you know."

"I saw her down the hall just now. She was with her son."

"Yes. I guess Sue called Louise's son as soon as the ambulance left. He must have come right over. He's been here for about half an hour now, trying to comfort his mother. Such a nice young man!"

Darcy reached out and touched Helen-Marie's shoulder. "Thanks for filling me in. I'm going on down and talk to Louise. Maybe there's something I can do."

When Darcy reached the end of the hall, Sue and Zeke were helping Louise back toward her room. "I heard what happened," Darcy said as she joined them. "I'm so sorry." She reached out and took Louise's hand. "Any word from the hospital yet?"

"Nothing yet," Zeke said as he helped his mother into her room. "But as soon as Mom is settled here, I think I'll go over to the hospital myself and see how Wadsworth is doing."

Sue looked up at him, the worried look never leaving her face. "Before you do, why don't I give them a call? Maybe by now they'll be able to tell me something." She turned toward Darcy. "I tried a while ago, but they weren't able to give me any sort of report yet. Maybe now. . . ." She helped Louise into a chair and then turned toward the door. "I'll see what I can find out—be back in a minute."

Louise buried her face in her hands and began sobbing quietly.

"Mom," Zeke said softly, his concern apparent, "maybe he'll be okay. People do recover from heart attacks, you know."

Louise nodded. "I know they do." She reached

out and took her son's hand. "But Wadsworth's not a young man anymore. He's eighty-one."

"I can understand why you're worried, Mrs. Ryan," Darcy said softly. "But remember, Zeke is right. Wadsworth may still be okay. So don't give up hope yet."

Sue came back into the room. "I've got some news. Not a lot, but what there is I think may be good."

They watched her anxiously.

"He's in intensive care now. They're watching him closely, but at the present time he's holding his own. They're what I'd call guardedly optimistic."

Louise sighed deeply as she reached for a tissue. "I'm so glad to hear that," she said softly.

"It's no guarantee, of course," Sue said as she watched Louise, "but at least it's a step in the right direction."

Louise wiped her eyes. "Honestly, I just don't know what I'd do if anything happened to Wadsworth. He's brought so much joy to my life." She reached for another tissue. "He's given a new meaning to everything."

Zeke gave his mother's hands a squeeze, and Darcy quickly said a silent prayer that Wadsworth would come through this all right. It looked like Zeke was finally getting over his uneasiness about the engagement and maybe even beginning to understand how very much Wadsworth meant to his mother.

She heard some footsteps in the hall and looked toward the door. Luke stepped into the room. "Hello, everybody," he said as he came over and, after lightly touching Darcy's shoulder, reached down and gently took Louise's hand in his. "I just came from the hospital. I saw Wadsworth briefly, and all things considered, I'd say he's doing pretty well."

"I just called," Sue said. "They told me he's in ICU."

Luke nodded. "Yes. Of course, that's the best place for him right now. I had a short talk with the cardiologist before I left." He sat down next to Louise. "He said Wadsworth was responding well, and that, in view of everything, he thought he had a pretty strong heart."

"I'm so glad to hear that, Doctor," Louise said, looking up gratefully at Luke.

"They've got a great cardiac team over there at St. Elizabeth. He couldn't be in a better place."

Zeke stood up. "I was thinking of running over there. Do you think I could get to see him, even for a minute?"

Luke shook his head. "I very much doubt it, Zeke. But even so, it might not be a bad idea for you to stop in. You can talk to one of the nurses, maybe get a firsthand report yourself. And I know it will make Wadsworth feel good when they tell him you stopped by."

Zeke slipped on his coat. "Why don't I do that, then? Is that okay with you, Mom?"

Louise nodded. "It would be wonderful, dear. Just as Dr. Randall said, it would mean a lot to Wadsworth—and also to me."

Zeke kissed her on the cheek and went out the door.

Later that afternoon Darcy and Luke sat at a table at the far end of the deserted cafeteria.

"This coffee is really awful," Darcy said with a grimace. The kitchen staff hadn't brewed coffee for dinner yet, and all that was available was a grayish liquid from a coin-operated machine. "I ought to know better than to buy this stuff."

Luke stirred his own coffee absently. "We both should—by now."

Darcy looked across at him. "I'm so glad that Wadsworth's condition is at least considered stable."

Luke nodded. "Of course he's not out of the woods yet, but who knows—he may just pull through."

"It would be awful for Louise if something happened to him. I don't know if she could handle it."

"I agree. It could be very hard on her."

"Isn't it sad—that at the very time in life when people have to suffer from so many infirmities, illnesses, pain, things like that, that they also have to go through these other losses? Like Louise, possibly losing Wadsworth, at a time when they both need each other so much."

"It really is. I've thought of that a lot since I've been in geriatrics. It always tears me apart. I know doctors aren't supposed to get involved that way, but sometimes you just can't help it. It seems so unfair somehow."

"I hope that doesn't happen to Louise. Because I think she and Wadsworth are truly in love. She's almost eighty. It would be so hard on her to lose him now."

Luke reached out and took Darcy's hand. "I agree with you. Louise and Wadsworth love each other just as much, just as deeply, and just as romantically as any other engaged couple."

"People have such a hard time accepting that sometimes."

He sighed. "I know they do—like Zeke. I can see he's had some trouble with this whole thing between his mother and Wadsworth. But after this, after seeing the way Wadsworth's heart attack has affected his mother, I think maybe he'll understand the whole thing better. Then maybe he'll realize that we younger people don't have a monopoly on falling in love—that with Wadsworth and Louise, it's exactly the same way as it is with him and Sue." He hesitated and then lowered his voice. "Or with you and me, for that matter. Same feelings, same intensity—everything." He looked quickly around the deserted cafeteria and then, with a conspiratorial smile, he leaned across the table and kissed her on the lips. "I love you, Darcy Lewis. And if I haven't said it before, well, it's high time that I did."

Darcy looked at him in surprise. He usually took every precaution to conduct himself professionally, and the impulsive kiss was completely out of character. Even so, she was delighted, and for the first time that day, her face broke into a huge smile. "And I love you too, Luke," she said softly. And she did. In a way that she had never thought possible, she knew that she loved this man with all her heart. He was everything she had ever dreamed of.

He reached out and gave her hand a squeeze. "We'll talk more later." He looked around the still-empty cafeteria. "I guess this is hardly the place. Anyway, I've got to get back to the hospital. I'll stop by and see how Wadsworth's doing." He stood up and slipped on his coat. "Maybe, with luck, this whole thing will have a happy ending, after all." He leaned down and kissed her one more time and then turned and headed quickly across the deserted room and out the door.

Chapter Nine

On the morning before Thanksgiving, Roy Bogan sat in his wheelchair in a corner of the Good Shepherd dayroom, absently petting Odysseus. At the far end of the room, two of the aides were putting up decorations.

"Hi, Mr. Bogan," Darcy called as she came briskly across the empty room. "We were just getting ready to start the book-discussion group, but then we realized that you weren't there. Aren't you planning to join us this morning?"

"Oh, hello there, Darcy," Roy said, looking up. "No, as a matter of fact, I thought maybe I'd just skip the group today. You know, Pete brought Odysseus over to visit this morning—said he'd pick him up again about noon."

Darcy pulled a chair up and sat down. "Yes, I know. Fidella Ross told me." Earlier, Fidella had explained to Darcy that, since the next day was Thanksgiving, causing the shelter's regularly scheduled Thursday visit to be canceled, Pete had dropped Odysseus off for a few hours this morning.

"Pete thought it would be good for Roy to have the time with Odysseus that he otherwise would miss," Fidella had explained. "You know how Roy looks forward to those visits."

Darcy agreed that indeed he did, and she remarked on how thoughtful it was of Pete to take the extra time to bring the cat over. The way things were turning out, she thought, spending time with Odysseus had become the center of Roy's life.

Darcy reached over and gently scratched Odysseus's ear. "If you want, I could wheel you both down to the discussion group. I don't think the others would mind if Odysseus came along, just this once."

Roy looked up at her and smiled contentedly. "Oh, I think I'm just going to skip it today, Darcy, if you don't mind. I kind of enjoy being here alone with Odysseus." He continued to gently stroke the cat. "It's a nice change from all the usual hustle and bustle."

Darcy stood up. "Well, okay—if you're really sure."

"I'm sure, Darcy," he said as he continued contentedly petting the sleeping Odysseus.

Later, after the book-discussion group was over, Darcy stopped in to say good-bye before heading over to Towering Oaks. But Roy had dozed off in his wheelchair while Odysseus, curled into a sleek, tiny ball, purred noisily in his lap.

"Everyone's so excited!" Sue said when Darcy arrived at Towering Oaks that afternoon. "We've never had a wedding here before!"

"I'm pretty excited myself! This is a once-in-a-lifetime event."

Sue sighed. "Isn't it wonderful, the way things are turning out? Everything's happening according to schedule, after all."

Darcy nodded. "In fact, Luke thinks that part of Wadsworth's speedy recovery may be due to his knowing that Louise was back here, waiting for him."

"I wouldn't be surprised." Sue smiled happily. "Isn't love wonderful?"

Darcy looked at her and then reached out to give her friend a quick hug. "It sure is," she said softly. "It makes everything worthwhile." She hung up her coat and then turned back to face Sue. "So, you and Zeke will be standing up for the happy couple tomorrow?"

"Right. I've got my dress and everything. It's a gorgeous blue."

"And Louise?"

"She's wearing a lovely silk print. The dressmaker was in this morning, shortening it a bit for her."

"What about Wadsworth? Is he all set?"

"I guess he is. Zeke helped him get a handsome new navy-blue suit for the occasion."

"It all sounds wonderful."

"That's because it is. And, by the way, Zeke is really happy about the way things have turned out. Remember all those doubts he had a month or so ago—before Wadsworth's heart attack?"

Darcy nodded.

"Well, they're all gone now. He thinks this is the greatest thing that could have happened. He's genuinely happy for his mother."

Darcy smiled. "With time, I think we both knew that he'd come around. What he was feeling at first—the uneasiness and all—I think that was pretty standard under the circumstances. Incidentally, did things finally work out so that Wadsworth and Louise will get a room together, the way they wanted?"

Sue nodded happily. "Not only that—they'll have one of the nicest rooms here—104. It's down at the far end of the west corridor. It costs a little more, but Zeke and also Wadsworth's daughter and son-in-law have agreed to pick up the difference."

"Then everything really is working out all right, isn't it? The big question left now is about you and Zeke." Darcy lowered her voice. "Any chance of another wedding—maybe around Christmas?"

Sue laughed. "Not quite that soon, but—well, who knows? Maybe by spring."

"Terrific!" Darcy slung her canvas bag over her shoulder and started down the hall.

"Just a minute!" Sue called after her. Darcy turned back to face her. "The way things are looking to me, there could be still a third wedding brewing in the future. How about it?"

"Why, Sue, whatever could you mean?" Darcy said with exaggerated innocence.

Sue grinned. "Don't give me that cat-that-just-swallowed-the-canary smile, Darcy Lewis! You know darned well what I mean—you and Luke! Things are beginning to look pretty serious there too."

Darcy turned once more toward the seminar room. "You just may be right, Sue," she called over her shoulder. "It's feeling kind of serious to me too."

"I am so full—I don't think I'll ever want to eat another thing." Luke leaned forward and put his plate on the large oak coffee table in front of the blazing fire. "First that great turkey dinner over at Towering Oaks and now this." He turned sideways on the sofa and smiled appreciatively at Darcy. "To be sure, it was the best apple pie

I ever had." He reached over and gently brushed away a curl that hovered near the side of her face. "But enough is enough."

His touch felt warm and loving, and Darcy sighed contentedly as she moved closer to him. "It really was a terrific dinner, wasn't it?" she said softly. "The staff outdid themselves today."

"Not only that—the whole day was remarkable." He gently pulled her closer to him. "A beautiful wedding and a very happy occasion."

"I'll never forget it," Darcy said softly, nestling her head on his shoulder. "Even at age eighty, I don't think any bride could have been prettier than Louise."

"You're right." He lightly kissed the top of her head. "Louise was lovely. But then old Wadsworth didn't look so bad, either—especially considering all he's gone through. After all, he had a really close call with that heart attack—closer, perhaps, than anyone, including Wadsworth himself, realizes."

"Well, he looked very handsome. Even in his wheelchair, he sat up straight and looked extremely dignified." She sighed. "It was all just gorgeous."

"It was also good having all the other residents there too. Something like this gives everyone a big lift. I've heard of marriages happening in retirement homes before, but they certainly don't happen too often. When they do, they're always happy occasions."

"And it was nice the way they had Zeke and Sue stand up for them."

"That was a good touch. They're a great couple. I'm glad things seem to be working out so well for them."

"It's just a matter of time," Darcy said happily. "You wait and see. We'll be having another wedding by Easter—maybe even sooner."

"Well, since you've brought it up. . . ." He moved forward on the couch as he turned to face her. "I've been thinking. . . ."

Darcy looked up at him. "Yes?" she asked softly. She was pretty sure she knew what he was going to say, and, deep inside, her heart began turning cartwheels as she watched him.

"Speaking of weddings. . . ." He began fumbling in his pocket. "I just happen to have something here." He pulled out a tiny white box and held it in his hand. "You see, all this talk about people falling in love and getting married—well, it got me to thinking." He grinned mischievously at her. "And I thought to myself, 'I love this woman'—meaning you, of course—'I love this woman very much.' And then I asked myself, 'Well, if you love her so much, what, exactly, are you going to do about it?' "

Darcy smiled up at him happily. "And what,"

she asked with exaggerated formality, "did you answer yourself?"

"I answered myself. . . ." And without finishing the sentence, he leaned forward and gently placed his lips on hers. "I answered myself—this." And he placed the tiny white box into her hand.

With trembling hands, she opened the lid. A thin gold ring, set with one exquisite diamond, gleamed out at her. She caught her breath. "Oh, Luke, it's gorgeous!"

Gently he took the ring out of the box and slipped it on her finger. Then, taking her hand in both of his, he smiled down at her. "Say you'll marry me, Darcy." He leaned forward and kissed her lightly on the lips. "I love you very much—more than I ever dreamed possible."

Almost automatically Darcy let her free arm creep up and around his neck. "And I love you too," she said softly as her arm tightened around his neck. "Of course I'll marry you."

He smiled and then kissed her again. Finally he leaned back on the sofa and, wrapping both arms tightly around her, pulled her to him. "We can have a great life together, sweetheart," he said softly as he gazed at the blazing fire. "I know now that I want to make geriatrics my medical specialty. And who knows? Maybe we could go into practice together. After all, you're both a

nurse and a trained gerontologist. That's a dyna-
mite combination. And, incidentally, you're so
good in that field. I've watched the patients inter-
act with you. They all just love you." He gave
her a tiny squeeze. "But then, who wouldn't?"

Darcy smiled up at him. "I'll bet you say that
to all the—"

"To all the gerontologists I meet?" He grinned
down at her. "Yes, as a matter of fact, I do. I
meet so many of them, you know. That's always
my standard opening."

"Silly," she said softly.

He leaned forward and kissed her again. "Anyway, when I'm not out pursuing all these gerontologists that I meet, you know what I'm doing?"

"What?"

"I'm thinking about you—and how very much
I love you."

She looked up at him, and their eyes locked.
"I love you too, Luke," she said softly. "And I
would very much like to share the rest of my life
with you." He gave her a gentle hug, and they
sat for several minutes contentedly watching the
fire. "Incidentally," she said finally, "I also think
you're a wonderful doctor—even," she added
slyly, "if your ideas about my writing group were
a bit strange at first."

Luke threw back his head and laughed.
"You're never going to let me forget that, are

you?" He grinned down at her. "Okay—so I went off the deep end a bit there at first."

"A bit?"

"Well, a small amount," he said sheepishly. "Let's just say I overreacted." He kissed the top of her head. "The writing group is fine. It's one of the best programs Towering Oaks has ever had." He kissed her again. "So there!"

"You know something?" Darcy said looking up at him.

"What?"

"You and I—I think we're going to have a great life together."

"I know we will."

He held her close, his cheek resting lightly on the top of her head. "Hey, I just noticed something." Darcy looked up at him. He was gazing toward the opposite window. "I think it's snowing out."

She looked toward the window. A slanted stream of hard, white snow whipped past the window, picking up the reflected light from the living-room lamp. "That looks like serious snow," Darcy said softly.

He looked down at her. "Serious snow? As opposed to unserious snow?"

Darcy laughed. "No—well, maybe. Anyway, that's what Grandma used to say. She used to call snow like that—when it blew in a stream sort of

sideways and the flakes were narrow and thin—
'serious snow.' But those big fat flakes. . . ." She
made a circle with her thumb and middle finger.
"You know, the kind that just sort of flop lazily
around in the air? Grandma would call that 'play
snow.' It was fun to play in, she'd tell me, but
it wasn't going to amount to a hill of beans." She
looked up at him. "And you know what? Most
of the time, she was right."

"So that"—he nodded toward the window—
"that is what you'd call serious snow."

Darcy looked again. "Yes. I think that can
properly be called serious snow."

"Meaning we could get snowed in here."

She looked up at him. "I doubt that, but—"

"But you never know."

She smiled. "Right."

"So maybe, if I don't want to get snowed in
here with you, I ought to think about heading on
back to my place. Before that serious snow starts
making the roads impassable."

She watched him quietly, trying to suppress a
smile. "I suppose you could say that," she said
evenly.

"But then, on the other hand, if it just so happened that I wouldn't mind getting snowed in
here with you, then I guess there wouldn't be any
big hurry."

"I suppose you could say that too," Darcy

said, still trying to keep a solemn look on her face.

"Well, then"—he turned back to face the fireplace as he wrapped both arms tightly around her—"I think I'll just stay put for a while."

Darcy snuggled contentedly up against him as she let her head rest on his shoulder. "I think that sounds like a very good idea," she said softly.

And for a long time they sat quietly together, watching the flickering fire and dreaming about the future while the whirling snow continued to drift against the living-room window.